William Edmondstoune Aytoun

Lays of the Scottish Cavaliers and Other Poems

William Edmondstoune Aytoun

Lays of the Scottish Cavaliers and Other Poems

ISBN/EAN: 9783744716604

Printed in Europe, USA, Canada, Australia, Japan

Cover: Foto ©Andreas Hilbeck / pixelio.de

More available books at **www.hansebooks.com**

Companion Poets

LAYS

OF THE

SCOTTISH CAVALIERS

AND OTHER POEMS

BY

WILLIAM EDMONDSTOUNE AYTOUN

PROFESSOR OF RHETORIC AND BELLES LETTRES
IN THE UNIVERSITY OF EDINBURGH

WITH

AN INTRODUCTION BY HENRY MORLEY, LL.D.

LONDON
GEORGE ROUTLEDGE & SONS, LIMITED
BROADWAY, LUDGATE HILL,
GLASGOW, MANCHESTER, AND NEW YORK
1891

INTRODUCTION.

—◦§◦—

WILLIAM EDMONDSTOUNE AYTOUN, says the friend
of kindred genius, Sir Theodore Martin, who in
1867 paid to him just honour by writing a Memoir
of his life, was descended from the scholar and
poet, Sir Robert Aytoun, of whom Ben Jonson was
loved dearly, as he told Drummond of Hawthorn-
den, and whom Hobbes of Malmesbury "made
use of for an Aristarchus, when he made his epistle
dedicatory for his translation of 'Thucydides.'"
Burns took the idea of his "Auld Lang Syne"
from Sir Robert Aytoun's poem beginning

> " Should old acquaintance be forgot
> And never thought upon."

The father of William Edmondstoune Aytoun
was Roger Aytoun, partner at Edinburgh in a
leading firm of Writers to the Signet. Roger
Aytoun was a cultivated man, a Whig, and a
friend of Francis Jeffrey. He was married to a
lady who had beauty, piety, and love of romance
—a Jacobite who, when a girl, had seen Walter
Scott in his boyhood, who delighted in the ballad
poetry of Scotland, and transmitted her tastes to
her only son.

William Edmondstoune Aytoun, born in June
1813, was the only son of these parents; but he
had two sisters, both of whom survived him, and
to whom his friend dedicated his Memoir. Aytoun
as a child was quick-witted, quick-tempered, and

5

ready at fun. When ten or eleven years old he
read with keen relish Scott's novels, and was glad
to lay hold of the "Devil on Two Sticks," or
"Humphrey Clinker." As a schoolboy he was
full of animal spirits, too bright to be among the
dunces, but only getting enough Latin and Greek
to enable him to keep a fair place among school-
boys. His livelier sense of Latin and its literature,
as something real and enjoyable, he got at the
Edinburgh University from Professor Pillans. He
advanced less in Greek, though drawn especially
to Homer. He wrote much verse; serious verse
in the manner of Pope and Dryden, ballads and
squibs after his own lively fashion. He delighted
also in field sports, and relished joyously the intercourse with friends. It was at college that Theodore Martin, also a student, but a few years
Aytoun's junior, first saw him, when he was
cleverly upsetting with an effective, unpremeditated
speech the effect of the forced oratory of leaders
in a students' meeting. That was in 1832, when
Aytoun's age was seventeen, and in the same year
his sympathy with the cause of the Poles led to his
publishing "Poland, Homer, and other Poems."

In the following year Aytoun came to London,
and spent several months in the chambers of a
busy solicitor and parliamentary agent. He satisfied himself that there would not be a career for
him as barrister in London, and spent the next
winter at Aschaffenburg for acquisition of the
German language and a study of its literature
under Professor J. E. Merkel. There he translated the first part of *Faust* into English verse,
and he wished to publish the translation. At
the same time, while urging his disinclination and
unfitness against his father's wish that he should
be a Writer to the Signet, he indicated the Chair
of Belles Lettres in the University as a suitable
object of ambition, for which he might fit himself
by literary studies. Aytoun's translation of *Faust*
never was published. When he returned to Edin-

burgh in April 1834, he found no fewer than four
new translations of *Faust*, either published or
announced as in the press. Aytoun delighted
also in the German fun and the bright poetical
fancy of Tieck, and was stimulated by his contact
with the German mind to much literary activity.
But as Law seemed to be the only profession open
to him, he passed the necessary examinations, was
admitted in 1835 as Writer to the Signet, and
worked in the chambers of his father's firm. But
its business declined, and Aytoun resolved to try
his fortune at the Scottish Bar, to which he was
called in 1840. His known pursuit of literature
did him no good with the solicitors. He had
published in *Blackwood* translations from Uhland,
and had translated the 22nd book of the "Iliad"
into English trochaics. In November 1839 his
poem of "Hermotimus" had appeared in *Blackwood;* in May 1840 he published, in *Blackwood*,
translations from the Romaic ; and in December
1841, also in *Blackwood*, his poem of "Blind
Old Milton." In 1840, also, his "Life and
Times of Richard the First" appeared in the
series of the "Family Library." As a barrister he
did get, however, a moderate share of work, and
did it well, especially criminal business, upon the
Western Circuit.

By the wit, fun, and bright sense of literature
which give permanent life to the caricatures of the
Bon Gaultier Ballads, Theodore Martin first drew
Aytoun to his side. The Bon Gaultier Ballads,
which his new friend had begun to contribute to
the magazines, tickled his fancy, and when he
found that it was proposed to produce more, he
undertook to join in their production. "In this
way," says his biographer, "a kind of Beaumont
and Fletcher partnership commenced in a series
of humorous papers, which appeared in *Tait's* and
Fraser's Magazines during the years 1842, 1843,
and 1844. In these papers, in which we ran
a-tilt, with all the recklessness of youthful spirits,

against such of the tastes or follies of the day as
presented an opening for ridicule or mirth, at the
same time that we did not altogether lose sight
of a purpose higher than mere amusement, appeared the verses, with a few exceptions, which
subsequently became popular, to a degree we
then little contemplated, as the 'Bon Gaultier
Ballads.'" The whimsical imitations in these
ballads of the manner of many poets was far in
advance of the mere fun of the "Rejected Ad-
dresses." It was possible only to men of high
spirits, with eager relish for literature and a living
sense of it, who in sympathy with men of genius
might feel, each for himself, "Auch ich war in
Arkadien geboren." "It was precisely the poets
whom we most admired," says Theodore Martin,
"that we imitated the most frequently. Let no
one parody a poet unless he loves him. He must
first be penetrated by his spirit, and have steeped
his ear in the music of his verse, before he can reflect these under a humorous aspect with success."

In pleasant differences lies much of the charm
of friendship, and with the poetry in Aytoun's
nature there had grown from his first lessons at
his mother's knee a romantic cavalier attachment
to the Stuarts ; a historical faith which, says his
friend, "was to him only less sacred than his
religious creed." His Scottish attachment to the
Stuarts, "was so real that it coloured his views
of the history of that dynasty and its followers to
a degree which surprised those who knew how
critical was his observation and how practical his
judgment in all other matters. Touch this theme
at any time, even when his flow of mirthful spirits
was at its fullest, and his tremulous voice and
quivering lip told how deeply-seated were his
feelings in all that related to it. On any other
point he would bear to be rallied, but not upon
this." Nettled by Thackeray's just treatment of
Mary Stuart in one of his "Lectures on the
Four Georges," when those lectures were given at

Edinburgh, Aytoun said to him with unwonted harshness, "Stick to your Jeameses, Thackeray! They are more in your line than the Georges." The knowledge of this feeling in Aytoun will put some of the requisite heartiness into the reading of this book of his best serious verse, the "Lays of the Scottish Cavaliers." The first of his ballads, which obtained for him the first success in serious verse, was the "Burial March of Dundee," which appeared in *Blackwood's Magazine* for April 1843. When he wrote it his father was dying, and his father died not many days before its publication. His father's death left Aytoun free, without home antagonism, to take his natural side as a party writer. He could only be a Conservative in politics.

In few cases did Aytoun make a more effective use of his powers than in the earnest humour of his protest against the disastrous Railway Mania, entitled "How we got up the Glenmutchkin Railway, and how we got out of it."

In 1845 the removal of Professor Spalding to St. Andrew's left vacant the chair of Rhetoric and Belles Lettres in the University of Edinburgh. As a student in Germany he had named to his father this chair as an object of ambition. Literature was the work for which he was most fit. He had been toiling at the Bar with slow success, while gradually earning his good name among writers. The salary attached to the chair was only £100, and the annual income from fees did not exceed £130. He obtained the chair, and raised the number of the students from thirty in 1846 to upwards of 150 in 1864. He had also before his appointment become, as a contributor, intimately connected with *Blackwood's Magazine*, and for many years after 1844 wrote for it almost monthly. In April 1849 Aytoun was married to the youngest daughter of Professor Wilson, and it was only then that he ceased to reside with his mother and sisters. When Lord Derby came into office in 1852 a vacancy in the sheriffship of Orkney and Zetland enabled him to requite with that office Aytoun's political services. Aytoun punctually fulfilled his duties, and usually spent in the Orkneys a part of the summer months. In June 1853 Professor Aytoun received from Oxford the honorary degree of D.C.L.

In May 1854 there appeared in *Blackwood* Aytoun's sham criticism of an unpublished tragedy, "Firmilian," by Percy Jones. The criticism and the extracts were both from one hand, but they took in many of the critics, and Aytoun was led to crown his joke by publishing a complete tragedy of "Firmilian," in caricature of the spasmodic style. At the end of 1855 Aytoun began to write his "Bothwell," which was published in the following year, and with which he was never himself satisfied. Then, after a few months' rest from literary labour, he was hard at work again. In 1857 he prepared an edition of Scottish Ballads. In 1858 he was busy with his friend, Theodore Martin, upon a reprint of their translation of Goethe's Ballads and minor poems, which had appeared in *Blackwood* in 1843-44. In April 1859 Aytoun's wife died, leaving him childless. "Night after night," says Mr. John Blackwood, "I used to call in upon him, and anything more melancholy than our old bright companion, sitting with his head leaning on his hands, cheerless and helpless, I never saw."

After this time Aytoun's health broke. He began to publish in *Blackwood* his novel of "Norman Sinclair," diffuse and ill-arranged, but full of good thought and covert personal reminiscence. He was sleepless and plagued with dyspepsia, in which, as he painted its agonies, "a mutton chop becomes a fiery crab, rending the interior with its claws; and even rice-pudding has the intolerable effrontery to become revivified as a hedgehog." In 1861 he sought health at the baths at Homburg. In November of that year his mother died, at the age

of ninety. In 1862 he went again to Homburg.
He had grown thinner, and there was hectic flush
upon his cheek. After this time he wrote but
little. He sought comfort in a second marriage in
December 1863, was happy in it, and improved
in health till, in the winter of 1864, the old dis-
tressing symptoms recurred. Next year he tried
summer quarters in Scotland ; in June 1865 wrote
a vigorous political article for *Blackwood*. But on
the 4th of the next August he died, sinking so
rapidly that his sisters, summoned by telegram
from Edinburgh, did not arrive till some hours
after his death. "We went straight to his room,"
writes one of them, "and there he lay like a
statue, with a heavenly smile upon his lips, and
the colour in his cheek. It did not look like
death ; and they had laid him out with bunches of
his favourite white roses on his breast."

H. M.

CONTENTS.

Lays of the Scottish Cavaliers.

Miscellaneous Poems.

Lays of
The Scottish Cavaliers

—⚬⚭⚬—

Edinburgh after Flodden.

THE great battle of Flodden was fought upon the 9th of September 1513. The defeat of the Scottish army, mainly owing to the fantastic ideas of chivalry entertained by James IV., and his refusal to avail himself of the natural advantages of his position, was by far the most disastrous of any recounted in the history of the northern wars. The whole strength of the kingdom, both Lowland and High-land, was assembled, and the contest was one of the sternest and most desperate upon record.

For several hours the issue seemed doubtful. On the left the Scots obtained a decided advantage; on the right wing they were broken and overthrown; and at last the whole weight of the battle was brought into the centre, where King James and the Earl of Surrey commanded in person. The determined valour of James, imprudent as it was, had the effect of rousing to a pitch of desperation the courage of the meanest soldiers; and the ground becoming soft and slippery from blood, they pulled off their boots and shoes, and secured a firmer footing by fighting in their hose.

"It is owned," says Abercromby, "that both parties did wonders, but none on either side performed more than the King himself. He was

15

again told that by coming to handy blows he
could do no more than another man, whereas, by
keeping the post due to his station, he might be
worth many thousands. Yet he would not only
fight in person, but also on foot; for he no sooner
saw that body of the English give way which was
defeated by the Earl of Huntly, but he alighted
from his horse, and commanded his guard of
noblemen and gentlemen to do the like and follow
him. He had at first abundance of success; but
at length the Lord Thomas Howard and Sir
Edward Stanley, who had defeated their opposites,
coming in with the Lord Dacre's horse, and sur-
rounding the King's battalion on all sides, the
Scots were so distressed that, for their last defence,
they cast themselves into a ring; and being resolved to die nobly with their sovereign, who
scorned to ask quarter, were altogether cut off.
So say the English writers, and I am apt to believe
that they are in the right."

The combat was maintained with desperate fury
until nightfall. At the close, according to Mr.
Tytler, "Surrey was uncertain of the result of the
battle: the remains of the enemy's centre still held
the field; Home with his Borderers still hovered
on the left; and the commander wisely allowed
neither pursuit nor plunder, but drew off his men,
and kept a strict watch during the night. When
the morning broke, the Scottish artillery were seen
standing deserted on the side of the hill; their
defenders had disappeared; and the Earl ordered
thanks to be given for a victory which was no
longer doubtful. Yet, even after all this, a body
of the Scots appeared unbroken upon a hill, and
were about to charge the Lord-Admiral, when they
were compelled to leave their position by a discharge of the English ordnance.

"The loss of the Scots in this fatal battle
amounted to about ten thousand men. Of these,
a great proportion were of high rank; the remainder being composed of the gentry, the

farmers, and landed yeomanry, who disdained
to fly when their sovereign and his nobles lay
stretched in heaps around them." Besides King
James, there fell at Flodden the Archbishop of
St. Andrews, thirteen earls, two bishops, two
abbots, fifteen lords and chiefs of clans, and
five peers' eldest sons, besides La Motte the
French ambassador, and the secretary of the
King. The same historian adds—"The names
of the gentry who fell are too numerous for re-
capitulation, since there were few families of note
in Scotland which did not lose one relative or
another, whilst some houses had to weep the
death of all. It is from this cause that the
sensations of sorrow and national lamentation
occasioned by the defeat were peculiarly poignant
and lasting—so that to this day few Scotsmen can
hear the name of Flodden without a shudder of
gloomy regret."

The loss to Edinburgh on this occasion was
peculiarly great. All the magistrates and able-
bodied citizens had followed their king to Flodden,
whence very few of them returned. The office of
Provost or chief magistrate of the capital was at
that time an object of ambition, and was conferred
only upon persons of high rank and station.
There seems to be some uncertainty whether the
holder of this dignity at the time of the battle of
Flodden was Sir Alexander Lauder, ancestor of the
Fountainhall family, who was elected in 1511, or
that great historical personage, Archibald Earl of
Angus, better known as Archibald Bell-the-Cat,
who was chosen in 1513, the year of the battle.
Both of them were at Flodden. The name of Sir
Alexander. Lauder appears upon the list of the
slain ; Angus was one of the survivors, but his
son, George, Master of Angus, fell fighting
gallantly by the side of King James. The city
records of Edinburgh, which commence about this
period, are not clear upon the point, and I am
rather inclined to think that the Earl of Angus

was elected to supply the place of Lauder. But
although the actual magistrates were absent, they
had formally nominated deputies in their stead.
I find, on referring to the city records, that "George
of Tours" had been appointed to officiate in the
absence of the Provost, and that four other persons
were selected to discharge the office of bailies
until the magistrates should return.

It is impossible to describe the consternation
which pervaded the whole of Scotland when the
intelligence of the defeat became known. In Edinburgh it was excessive. Mr. Arnot, in the history
of that city, says—

"The news of their overthrow in the field of
Flodden reached Edinburgh on the day after the
battle, and overwhelmed the inhabitants with grief
and confusion. The streets were crowded with
women seeking intelligence about their friends,
clamouring and weeping. Those who officiated
in absence of the magistrates proved themselves
worthy of the trust. They issued a proclamation,
ordering all the inhabitants to assemble in military
array for defence of the city, on the tolling of
the bell; and commanding, 'that all women, and
especially strangers, do repair to their work, and
·not be seen upon the street *clamorand and cryand;*
and that women of the better sort do repair to the
church and offer up prayers, at the stated hours,
for our Sovereign Lord and his army, and the
townsmen who are with the army.'"

Indeed, the council records bear ample evidence
of the emergency of that occasion. Throughout
the earlier pages, the word "Flowdoun" frequently
occurs on the margin, in reference to various
hurried orders for arming and defence; and there
can be no doubt that, had the English forces
attempted to follow up their victory, and attack
the Scottish capital, the citizens would have resisted to the last. But it soon became apparent
that the loss sustained by the English was so severe,
that Surrey was in no condition to avail himself of

the opportunity; and in fact, shortly afterwards, he was compelled to disband his army.

The references to the city banner, contained in the following poem, may require a word of explanation. It is a standard still held in great honour and reverence by the burghers of Edinburgh, having been presented to them by James III., in return for their loyal service in 1482. This banner, along with that of the Earl Marischal, still conspicuous in the Library of the Faculty of Advocates, was honourably brought back from Flodden, and certainly never could have been displayed in a more memorable field. Maitland says, with reference to this very interesting relic of antiquity—

"As a perpetual remembrance of the loyalty and bravery of the Edinburghers on the aforesaid occasion, the King granted them a banner or standard, with a power to display the same in defence of their king, country, and their own rights. This flag is kept by the Convener of the Trades; at whose appearance therewith, it is said that not only the artificers of Edinburgh are obliged to repair to it, but all the artisans or craftsmen within Scotland are bound to follow it, and fight under the Convener of Edinburgh as aforesaid."

No event in Scottish history ever took a more lasting hold of the public mind than the "woeful fight" of Flodden; and, even now, the songs and traditions which are current on the Border recall the memory of a contest unsullied by disgrace, though terminating in disaster and defeat.

EDINBURGH AFTER FLODDEN.

I.

News of battle!—news of battle!
  Hark! 'tis ringing down the street:
And the archways and the pavement
  Bear the clang of hurrying feet.
News of battle? Who hath brought it?
  News of triumph? Who should bring
Tidings from our noble army,
  Greetings from our gallant King?
All last night we watched the beacons
  Blazing on the hills afar,
Each one bearing, as it kindled
  Message of the opened war.
All night long the northern streamers
  Shot across the trembling sky:
Fearful lights, that never beckon
  Save when kings or heroes die.

II.

News of battle! Who hath brought it?
  All are thronging to the gate;
"Warder—warder! open quickly!
  Man—is this a time to wait?"
And the heavy gates are opened:
  Then a murmur long and loud,
And a cry of fear and wonder
  Bursts from out the bending crowd.
For they see in battered harness
  Only one hard-stricken man,
And his weary steed is wounded.
  And his cheek is pale and wan.

Spearless hangs a bloody banner
   In his weak and drooping hand—
God ! can that be Randolph Murray,
   Captain of the city band ?

III.

Round him crush the people, crying,
   " Tell us all—oh, tell us true !
Where are they who went to battle,
   Randolph Murray, sworn to you ?
Where are they, our brothers—children ?
   Have they met the English foe ?
Why art thou alone, unfollowed ?
   Is it weal, or is it woe ? "
Like a corpse the grisly warrior
   Looks from out his helm of steel ;
But no word he speaks in answer,
   Only with his armèd heel
Chides his weary steed, and onward
   Up the city streets they ride ;
Fathers, sisters, mothers, children,
   Shrieking, praying by his side.
" By the God that made thee, Randolph !
   Tell us what mischance hath come ; "
Then he lifts his riven banner,
   And the asker's voice is dumb.

IV.

The elders of the city
   Have met within their hall—
The men whom good King James had charged
   To watch the tower and wall.
" Your hands are weak with age," he said,
   " Your hearts are stout and true ;
So bide ye in the Maiden Town,
   While others fight for you.
My trumpet from the Border-side
   Shall send a blast so clear,
That all who wait within the gate
   That stirring sound may hear.

Or, if it be the will of heaven
    That back I never come,
And if, instead of Scottish shouts,
    Ye hear the English drum,—
Then let the warning bells ring out,
    Then gird you to the fray,
Then man the walls like burghers stout,
    And fight while fight you may.
'Twere better that in fiery flame
    The roofs should thunder down,
Than that the foot of foreign foe
    Should trample in the town!"

V.

Then in came Randolph Murray,—
    His step was slow and weak,
And, as he doffed his dinted helm,
    The tears ran down his cheek:
They fell upon his corslet,
    And on his mailèd hand,
As he gazed around him wistfully,
    Leaning sorely on his brand.
And none who then beheld him
    But straight were smote with fear,
For a bolder and a sterner man
    Had never couched a spear.
They knew so sad a messenger
    Some ghastly news must bring:
And all of them were fathers,
    And their sons were with the King.

VI.

And up then rose the Provost—
    A brave old man was he,
Of ancient name, and knightly fame,
    And chivalrous degree.
He ruled our city like a Lord
    Who brooked no equal here,
And ever for the townsmen's rights
    Stood up 'gainst prince and peer.

And he had seen the Scottish host
  March from the Borough-muir,
With music-storm and clamorous shout,
And all the din that thunders out
  When youth's of victory sure.
But yet a dearer thought had he,
  For, with a father's pride,
He saw his last remaining son
  Go forth by Randolph's side,
With casque on head and spur on heel,
  All keen to do and dare ;
And proudly did that gallant boy
  Dunedin's banner bear.
Oh woeful now was the old man's look,
  And he spake right heavily—
" Now, Randolph, tell thy tidings,
  However sharp they be !
Woe is written on thy visage,
  Death is looking from thy face :
Speak, though it be of overthrow—
  It cannot be disgrace ! "

VII.

Right bitter was the agony
  That wrong that soldier proud :
Thrice did he strive to answer,
  And thrice he groaned aloud.
Then he gave the riven banner
  To the old man's shaking hand,
Saying—" That is all I bring ye
  From the bravest of the land !
Ay ! ye may look upon it—
  It was guarded well and long,
By your brothers and your children,
  By the valiant and the strong.
One by one they fell around it,
  As the archers laid them low,
Grimly dying, still unconquered,
  With their faces to the foe.
Ay ! ye well may look upon it—
  There is more than honour there, !!

Else, be sure, I had not brought it
  From the field of dark despair.
Never yet was royal banner
  Steeped in such a costly dye;
It hath lain upon a bosom
  Where no other shroud shall lie.
Sirs! I charge you, keep it holy,
  Keep it as a sacred thing,
For the stain ye see upon it
  Was the life-blood of your King!"

VIII.

Woe, woe, and lamentation!
  What a piteous cry was there!
Widows, maidens, mothers, children,
  Shrieking, sobbing in despair!
Through the streets the death-word rushes,
  Spreading terror, sweeping on—
"Jesu Christ! our King has fallen—
  O great God, King James is gone!
Holy Mother Mary, shield us,
  Thou who erst didst lose thy Son!
O the blackest day for Scotland
  That she ever knew before!
O our King—the good, the noble,
  Shall we see him never more?
Woe to us and woe to Scotland!
  O our sons, our sons and men!
Surely some have 'scaped the Southron,
  Surely some will come again!"
Till the oak that fell last winter
  Shall uprear its shattered stem—
Wives and mothers of Dunedin—
  Ye may look in vain for them!

IX.

But within the Council Chamber
  All was silent as the grave,

Whilst the tempest of their sorrow
  Shook the bosoms of the brave.
Well indeed might they be shaken
  With the weight of such a blow :
He was gone—their prince, their idol,
  Whom they loved and worshipped so !
Like a knell of death and judgment
  Rung from heaven by angel hand,
Fell the words of desolation
  On the elders of the land.
Hoary heads were bowed and trembling,
  Withered hands were clasped and wrung :
God had left the old and feeble,
  He had ta'en away the young.

X.

Then the Provost he uprose,
  And his lip was ashen white,
But a flush was on his brow,
  And his eye was full of light.
" Thou hast spoken, Randolph Murray
  Like a soldier stout and true ;
Thou hast done a deed of daring
  Had been perilled but by few.
For thou hast not shamed to face us,
  Nor to speak thy ghastly tale,
Standing—thou, a knight and captain—
  Here, alive within thy mail !
Now, as my God shall judge me,
  I hold it braver done,
Than hadst thou tarried in thy place,
  And died above my son !
Thou needst not tell it : he is dead.
  God help us all this day !
But speak—how fought the citizens
  Within the furious fray ?
For, by the might of Mary,
  'Twere something still to tell
That no Scottish foot went backward
  When the Royal Lion fell ! "

B

XI.

" No one failed him ! He is keeping
    Royal state and semblance still ;
Knight and noble lie around him,
    Cold on Flodden's fatal hill.
Of the brave and gallant-hearted,
    Whom ye sent with prayers away,
Not a single man departed
    From his monarch yesterday.
Had you seen them, O my masters !
    When the night began to fall,
And the English spearmen gathered
    Round a grim and ghastly wall !
As the wolves in winter circle
    Round the leaguer on the heath,
So the greedy foe glared upward,
    Panting still for blood and death.
But a rampart rose before them,
    Which the boldest dared not scale ;
Every stone a Scottish body,
    Every step a corpse in mail !
And behind it lay our monarch
    Clenching still his shivered sword :
By his side Montrose and Athole,
    At his feet a southern lord.
All so thick they lay together,
    When the stars lit up the sky,
That I knew not who were stricken,
    Or who yet remained to die.
Few there were when Surrey halted,
    And his wearied host withdrew ;
None but dying men around me,
    When the English trumpet blew.
Then I stooped, and took the banner,
    As ye see it, from his breast,
And I closed our hero's eyelids,
    And I left him to his rest.
In the mountains growled the thunder,
    As I leaped the woeful wall,

And the heavy clouds were settling
  Over Flodden, like a pall."

XII.

So he ended.   And the others
  Cared not any answer then ;
Sitting silent, dumb with sorrow,
  Sitting anguish-struck, like men
Who have seen the roaring torrent
  Sweep their happy homes away,
And yet linger by the margin,
  Staring idly on the spray.
But, without, the maddening tumult
  Waxes ever more and more,
And the crowd of wailing women
  Gather round the Council door.
Every dusky spire is ringing
  With a dull and hollow knell,
And the Miserere's singing
  To the tolling of the bell.
Through the streets the burghers hurry,
  Spreading terror as they go ;
And the rampart's thronged with watchers
  For the coming of the foe.
From each mountain-top a pillar
  Streams into the torpid air,
Bearing token from the Border
  That the English host is there.
All without is flight and terror,
  All within is woe and fear—
God protect thee, Maiden City,
  For thy latest hour is near !

XIII.

No ! not yet, thou high Dunedin !
  Shalt thou totter to thy fall ;
Though thy bravest and thy strongest
  Are not there to man the wall.
No, not yet ! the ancient spirit
  Of our fathers hath not gone ;

Take it to thee as a buckler
  Better far than steel or stone.
Oh, remember those who perished
  For thy birthright at the time
When to be a Scot was treason,
  And to side with Wallace, crime!
Have they not a voice among us,
  Whilst their hallowed dust is here?
Hear ye not a summons sounding
  From each buried warrior's bier?
Up!—they say—and keep the freedom
  Which we won you long ago:
Up! and keep our graves unsullied
  From the insults of the foe!
Up! and if ye cannot save them,
  Come to us in blood and fire:
Midst the crash of falling turrets,
  Let the last of Scots expire!

XIV.

Still the bells are tolling fiercely,
  And the cry comes louder in;
Mothers wailing for their children,
  Sisters for their slaughtered kin.
All is terror and disorder,
  Till the Provost rises up,
Calm, as though he had not tasted
  Of the fell and bitter cup.
All so stately from his sorrow,
  Rose the old undaunted Chief,
That you had not deemed, to see him,
  His was more than common grief.
" Rouse ye, Sirs !" he said ; " we may not
  Longer mourn for what is done :
If our King be taken from us,
  We are left to guard his son.
We have sworn to keep the city
  From the foe, whate'er they be,
And the oath that we have taken
  Never shall be broke by me.

_ath is nearer to us, brethren,
   Than it seemed to those who died,
Fighting yesterday at Flodden,
   By their lord and master's side.
Let us meet it then in patience,
   Not in terror or in fear ;
Though our hearts are bleeding yonder,
   Let our souls be steadfast here.
Up, and rouse ye !   Time is fleeting,
   And we yet have much to do ;
Up ! and haste ye through the city,
   Stir the burghers stout and true !
Gather all our scattered people,
   Fling the banner out once more,—
Randolph Murray ! do thou bear it,
   As it erst was borne before :
Never Scottish heart will leave it,
   When they see their monarch's gore !

                    XV.

" Let them cease that dismal knelling !
   It is time enough to ring,   ·
When the fortress-strength of Scotland
   Stoops to ruin like its King.
Let the bells be kept for warning,
   Not for terror or alarm ;
When they next are heard to thunder,
   Let each man and stripling arm.
Bid the women leave their wailing,—
   Do they think that woeful strain,
From the bloody heaps of Flodden
   Can redeem their dearest slain ?
Bid them cease,—or rather hasten
   To the churches, every one ;
There to pray to Mary Mother,
   And to her anointed Son,
That the thunderbolt above us
   May not fall in ruin yet ;
That in fire, and blood, and rapine,
   Scotland's glory may not set.

Let them pray,—for never women
  Stood in need of such a prayer!
England's yeomen shall not find them
  Clinging to the altars there.
No! if we are doomed to perish,
  Man and maiden, let us fall;
And a common gulf of ruin
  Open wide to whelm us all!
Never shall the ruthless spoiler
  Lay his hot insulting hand
On the sisters of our heroes,
  Whilst we bear a torch or brand!
Up! and rouse ye, then, my brothers,—
  But when next ye hear the bell
Sounding forth the sullen summons
  That may be our funeral knell,
Once more let us meet together,
  Once more see each other's face;
Then, like men that need not tremble,
  Go to our appointed place.
God, our Father, will not fail us
  In that last tremendous hour,—
If all other bulwarks crumble,
  HE will be our strength and tower:
Though the ramparts rock beneath us,
  And the walls go crashing down,
Though the roar of conflagration
  Bellow o'er the sinking town;
There is yet one place of shelter,
  Where the foeman cannot come,
Where the summons never sounded
  Of the trumpet or the drum.
There again we'll meet our children,
  Who, on Flodden's trampled sod,
For their king and for their country
  Rendered up their souls to God.
There shall we find rest and refuge,
  With our dear departed brave;
And the ashes of the city
  Be our universal grave!"

THE EXECUTION OF MONTROSE.

THE most poetical chronicler would find it impossible to render the incidents of Montrose's brilliant career more picturesque than the reality. Among the devoted champions who, during the wildest and most stormy period of our history, maintained the cause of Church and King, "the Great Marquis" undoubtedly is entitled to the foremost place. Even party malevolence, by no means extinct at the present day, has been unable to detract from the eulogy pronounced upon him by the famous Cardinal de Retz, the friend of Condé and Turenne, when he thus summed up his character :—" Montrose, a Scottish nobleman, head of the house of Grahame—the only man in the world that has ever realised to me the ideas of certain heroes, whom we now discover nowhere but in the Lives of Plutarch—has sustained in his own country the cause of the King his master, with a greatness of soul that has not found its equal in our age."

But the success of the victorious leader and patriot is almost thrown into the shade by the noble magnanimity and Christian heroism of the man in the hour of defeat and death. Without wishing, in any degree, to revive a controversy long maintained by writers of opposite political and polemical opinions, it may fairly be stated that Scottish history does not present us with a tragedy of parallel interest. That the execution of Montrose was the natural, nay, the inevitable, consequence of his capture, may be freely admitted even by the fiercest partisan of the cause for which he staked his life. In those times, neither party was disposed to lenity; and Montrose was far too conspicuous a character, and too dangerous a man, to be forgiven. But the ignominious and savage treatment which he received at the hands of those whose station and descent should at least have taught them to respect misfortune, has left an indelible stain upon the memory of the Covenanting chiefs, and more especially upon that of Argyle.

The perfect serenity of the man in the hour of trial and death, the courage and magnanimity which he displayed to the last, have been dwelt upon with admiration by writers of every class. He heard his sentence delivered without any apparent emotion, and afterwards told the magistrates who waited upon him in prison, "that he was much indebted to the Parliament for the great honour they had decreed him;" adding, "that he was prouder to have his head placed upon the top of the prison, than if they had decreed a golden statue to be erected to him in the market-place, or that his picture should be hung in the King's bed-chamber." He said, "he thanked them for their care to preserve the remembrance of his loyalty, by transmitting such monuments to the different parts of the kingdom; and only wished that he had flesh enough to have sent a piece to every city in Christendom, as a token of his unshaken love and fidelity to his king and country." On the night before his execution, he inscribed the following lines with a diamond on the window of his jail :—

"Let them bestow on every airth a limb,
  Then open all my veins, that I may swim
To thee, my Maker! in that crimson lake;
Then place my parboiled head upon a stake—
Scatter my ashes—strew them in the air:
Lord! since thou know'st where all these atoms are,
I'm hopeful thou'lt recover once my dust,
And confident thou'lt raise me with the just."

After the Restoration, the dust *was* recovered, the scattered remnants collected, and the bones of the hero conveyed to their final resting-place by a numerous assemblage of gentlemen of his family and name.

There is no ingredient of fiction in the historical incidents recorded in the following ballad. The indignities that were heaped upon Montrose during his procession through Edinburgh, his appearance before the Estates, and his last passage to the scaffold, as well as his undaunted bearing, have all been spoken to by eye-witnesses of the scene. A graphic and vivid sketch of the whole will be found in Mr. Mark Napier's volume, "The Life and Times of Montrose"—a work as chivalrous in its tone as the Chronicles of Froissart, and abounding in original and most interesting materials; but, in order to satisfy all scruple, the authorities for each fact are given in the shape of notes. The ballad may be considered as a narrative of the transactions, related by an aged Highlander, who had followed Montrose throughout his campaigns, to his grandson, shortly before the battle of Killiecrankie.

THE EXECUTION OF MONTROSE.

I.

COME hither, Evan Cameron !
  Come, stand beside my knee—
I hear the river roaring down
  Towards the wintry sea.
There's shouting on the mountain side,
  There's war within the blast—
Old faces look upon me,
  Old forms go trooping past.
I hear the pibroch wailing
  Amidst the din of fight,
And my dim spirit wakes again
  Upon the verge of night !

II.

'Twas I that led the Highland host
  Through wild Lochaber's snows,
What time the plaided clans came down
  To battle with Montrose.
I've told thee how the Southrons fell
  Beneath the broad claymore,
And how we smote the Campbell clan
  By Inverlochy's shore.
I've told thee how we swept Dundee,
  And tamed the Lindsay's pride ;
But never have I told thee yet
  How the Great Marquis died !

III.

A traitor sold him to his foes ;
  O deed of deathless shame !

I charge thee, boy, if e'er thou meet
  With one of Assynt's name—
Be it upon the mountain's side,
  Or yet within the glen,
Stand he in martial gear alone,
  Or backed by armèd men—
Face him, as thou wouldst face the man
  Who wronged thy sire's renown ;
Remember of what blood thou art,
  And strike the caitiff down !

IV.

They brought him to the Watergate,
  Hard bound with hempen span,
As though they held a lion there,
  And not a fenceless man.
They set him high upon a cart—
  The hangman rode below—
They drew his hands behind his back,
  And bared his noble brow.
Then, as a hound is slipped from leash,
  They cheered the common throng,
And blew the note with yell and shout,
  And bade him pass along.

V.

It would have made a brave man's heart
  Grow sad and sick that day,
To watch the keen malignant eyes
  Bent down on that array.
There stood the Whig west-country lords
  In balcony and bow,
There sat their gaunt and withered dames,
  And their daughters all a-row ;
And every open window
  Was full as full might be,
With black-robed Covenanting carles,
  That goodly sport to see !

VI.

But when he came, though pale and wan,
    He looked so great and high,
So noble was his manly front,
    So calm his steadfast eye ;—-
The rabble rout forbore to shout,
    And each man held his breath,
For well they knew the hero's soul
    Was face to face with death.
And then a mournful shudder
    Through all the people crept,
And some that came to scoff at him,
    Now turn'd aside and wept.

VII.

But onwards—always onwards,
    In silence and in gloom,
The dreary pageant laboured,
    Till it reach'd the house of doom :
Then first a woman's voice was heard
    In jeer and laughter loud,
And an angry cry and a hiss arose
    From the heart of the tossing crowd :
Then, as the Græme looked upwards,
    He met the ugly smile
Of him who sold his King for gold—
    The master-fiend Argyle !

VIII.

The Marquis gazed a moment,
    And nothing did he say,
But the cheek of Argyle grew ghastly pale,
    And he turned his eyes away.
The painted harlot by his side,
    She shook through every limb,
For a roar like thunder swept the street,
    And hands were clenched at him,
And a Saxon soldier cried aloud,
    " Back, coward, from thy place !

For seven long years thou hast not dared
 To look him in the face."

IX.

Had I been there with sword in hand,
 And fifty Camerons by,
That day through high Dunedin's streets
 Had pealed the slogan cry.
Not all their troops of trampling horse,
 Nor might of mailèd men—
Not all the rebels of the south
 Had borne us backwards then !
Once more his foot on Highland heath
 Had trod as free as air,
Or I, and all who bore my name,
 Been laid around him there !

X.

It might not be. They placed him next
 Within the solemn hall,
Where once the Scottish Kings were throned
 Amidst their nobles all.
But there was dust of vulgar feet
 On that polluted floor,
And perjured traitors filled the place
 Where good men sate before.
With savage glee came Warristoun
 To read the murderous doom,
And then uprose the great Montrose
 In the middle of the room.

XI.

"Now by my faith as belted knight,
 And by the name I bear,
And by the bright Saint Andrew's cross
 That waves above us there—
Yea, by a greater, mightier oath—
 And oh, that such should be !—
By that dark stream of royal blood
 That lies 'twixt you and me—

I have not sought in battle-field
  A wreath of such renown,
Nor dared I hope, on my dying day,
  To win the martyr's crown !

XII.

" There is a chamber far away
  Where sleep the good and brave,
But a better place ye have named for me
  Than by my father's grave.
For truth and right, 'gainst treason's might,
  This hand hath always striven,
And ye raise it up for a witness still
  In the eye of earth and heaven.
Then nail my head on yonder tower—
  Give every town a limb—
And God who made shall gather them :
  I go from you to Him !"

XIII.

The morning dawned full darkly,
  The rain came flashing down,
And the jagged streak of the levin-bolt
  Lit up the gloomy town :
The heavens were thundering out their wrath,
  The fatal hour was come ;
Yet ever sounded sullenly
  The trumpet and the drum.
There was madness on the earth below,
  And anger in the sky,
And young and old, and rich and poor,
  Came forth to see him die.

XIV.

Ah, God ! that ghastly gibbet !
  How dismal 'tis to see
The great tall spectral skeleton,
  The ladder, and the tree !
Hark ! hark ! it is the clash of arms—
  The bells begin to toll—

He is coming! he is coming!
  God's mercy on his soul!
One last long peal of thunder—
  The clouds are cleared away,
And the glorious sun once more looks down
  Amidst the dazzling day.

XV.

He is coming! he is coming!
  Like a bridegroom from his room,
Came the hero from his prison
  To the scaffold and the doom.
There was glory on his forehead,
  There was lustre in his eye,
And he never walked to battle
  More proudly than to die:
There was colour in his visage,
  Though the cheeks of all were wan,
And they marvelled as they saw him pass,
  That great and goodly man!

XVI.

He mounted up the scaffold,
  And he turned him to the crowd;
But they dared not trust the people,
  So he might not speak aloud.
But he looked upon the heavens,
  And they were clear and blue,
And in the liquid ether
  The eye of God shone through:
Yet a black and murky battlement
  Lay resting on the hill,
As though the thunder slept within—
  All else was calm and still.

XVII.

The grim Geneva ministers
  With anxious scowl drew near,
As you have seen the ravens flock
  Around the dying deer.

He would not deign them word nor sign,
  But alone he bent the knee ;
And veiled his face for Christ's dear grace
  Beneath the gallows-tree.
Then radiant and serene he rose,
  And cast his cloak away :
For he had ta'en his latest look
  Of earth, and sun, and day.

XVIII.

A beam of light fell o'er him,
  Like a glory round the shriven,
And he climbed the lofty ladder
  As it were the path to heaven.
Then came a flash from out the cloud,
  And a stunning thunder roll,
And no man dared to look aloft,
  For fear was on every soul.
There was another heavy sound,
  A hush and then a groan ;
And darkness swept across the sky—
  The work of death was done !

NOTES TO "THE EXECUTION OF MONTROSE."

"*A traitor sold him to his foes,*" p. 34.

'The contemporary historian of the Earls of Sutherland records, that (after the defeat of Invercarron) Montrose and Kinnoull 'wandered up the river Kyle the whole ensuing night, and the next day, and the third day also, without any food or sustenance, and at last came within the country of Assynt. The Earl of Kinnoull, being faint for lack of meat, and not able to travel any further, was left there among the mountains, where it was supposed he perished. Montrose had almost famished, but that he fortuned in his misery to light upon a small cottage in that wilderness, where he was supplied with some milk and bread.' Not even the iron frame of Montrose could endure a prolonged existence under such circumstances. He gave himself up to Macleod of Assynt, a former adherent, from whom he had reason to expect assistance in consideration of that circumstance, and, indeed, from the dictates of honourable feeling and common humanity. As the Argyle faction had sold the King, so this Highlander rendered his own name infamous by selling the hero to the Covenanters, for which 'duty to the public' he was rewarded with four hundred bolls of meal."— NAPIER'S *Life of Montrose.*

"*They brought him to the Watergate,*" p. 35.

"*Friday,* 17*th May.* — Act ordaining James Grahame to be brought from the Watergate on

41

a cart, bareheaded, the hangman in his livery,
covered, riding on the horse that draws the cart—
the prisoner to be bound to the cart with a rope—
to the Tolbooth of Edinburgh, and from thence to
be brought to the Parliament House, and there, in
the place of delinquents, on his knees, to receive
his sentence—viz., to be hanged on a gibbet at the
Cross of Edinburgh, with his book and declaration
tied on a rope about his neck, and there to hang
for the space of three hours until he be dead ; and
thereafter to be cut down by the hangman, his
head, hands, and legs to be cut off, and distributed
as follows—viz., His head to be affixed on an iron
pin, and set on the pinnacle of the west gavel of
the new prison of Edinburgh ; one hand to be set
on the port of Perth, the other on the port of
Stirling ; one leg and foot on the port of Aberdeen,
the other on the port of Glasgow. If at his death
penitent, and relaxed from excommunication, then
the trunk of his body to be interred, by pioneers,
in the Greyfriars ; otherwise, to be interred in the
Boroughmuir, by the hangman's men, under the
gallows."—BALFOUR'S *Notes of Parliament.*

It is needless to remark that this inhuman
sentence was executed to the letter. In order that
the exposure might be more complete, the cart
was constructed with a high chair in the centre,
having holes behind, through which the ropes that
fastened him were drawn. The author of the
Wigton Papers, recently published by the Maitland
Club, says, "The reason of his being tied to the
cart was in hope that the people would have stoned
him, and that he might not be able by his hands
to save his face." His hat was then pulled off by
the hangman, and the procession commenced.

> "*But when he came, though pale and wan,*
> *He looked so great and high,*" *p.* 36.

"In all the way, there appeared in him such
majesty, courage, modesty—and even somewhat
more than natural—that those common women

who had lost their husbands and children in his
wars, and who were hired to stone him, were upon
the sight of him so astonished and moved, that
their intended curses turned into tears and prayers ;
so that next day *all the ministers preached against
them for not stoning and reviling him.*"—*Wigton
Papers.*

> " *Then first a woman's voice was heard
>   In jeer and laughter loud,*" *p.* 36.

"It is remarkable that, of the many thousand
beholders, the Lady Jean Gordon, Countess of
Haddington, did (alone) publicly insult and laugh
at him ; which being perceived by a gentleman in the
street, he cried up to her, that it became her better
to sit upon the cart for her adulteries."—*Wigton
Papers.* This infamous woman was the third
daughter of Huntly, and the niece of Argyle. It
will hardly be credited that she was the sister of
that gallant Lord Gordon, who fell fighting by the
side of Montrose, only five years before, at the
battle of Aldford !

> " *For seven long years thou hast not dared
>   To look him in the face,*" *p.* 37.

"The Lord Lorn and his new lady were also
sitting on a balcony, joyful spectators ; and the
cart being stopped when it came before the lodging
where the Chançellor, Argyle, and Warristoun
sat—that they might have time to insult—he,
suspecting the business, turned his face towards
them, whereupon they presently crept in at the
windows ; which being perceived by an English-
man, he cried up, it was no wonder they started
aside at his look, for they durst not look him in
the face these seven years bygone."—*Wigton
Papers.*

> " *With savage glee came Warristoun
>   To read the murderous doom,*" *p.* 37.

Archibald Johnston of Warristoun. This man,

who was the inveterate enemy of Montrose, and who carried the most selfish spirit into every intrigue of his party, received the punishment of his treasons about eleven years afterwards. It may be instructive to learn how *he* met his doom. The following extract is from the MSS. of Sir George Mackenzie :—" The Chancellor and others waited to examine him ; he fell upon his face, roaring, and with tears entreated they would pity a poor creature who had forgot all that was in the Bible. This moved all the spectators with a deep melancholy ; and the Chancellor, reflecting upon the man's great parts, former esteem, and the great share he had in all the late revolutions, could not deny some tears to the frailty of silly mankind. At his examination, he pretended he had lost so much blood by the unskilfulness of his chirurgeons, that he lost his memory with his blood ; and I really believe that his courage had been drawn out with it. Within a few days he was brought before the parliament, where he discovered nothing but much weakness, running up and down upon his knees, begging mercy ; but the parliament ordained his former sentence to be put to execution, and accordingly he was executed at the Cross of Edinburgh."

> " *And God who made shall gather them :*
> *I go from you to Him !*" p. 38.

" He said he was much beholden to the parliament for the honour they put on him ; ' for,' says he, ' I think it a greater honour to have my head standing on the port of this town, for this quarrel, than to have my picture in the king's bedchamber. I am beholden to you that, lest my loyalty should be forgotten, yé have appointed five of your most eminent towns to bear witness of it to posterity.' "
- *Wigton Papers.*

> " *He is coming ! he is coming !*
> *Like a bridegroom from his room,*" p. 39.

"In his downgoing from the Tolbooth to the place of execution, he was very richly clad in fine scarlet, laid over with rich silver lace, his hat in his hand, his bands and cuffs exceeding rich, his delicate white gloves on his hands, his stockings of incarnate silk, and his shoes with their ribbands on his feet; and sarks provided for him with pearling about, above ten pund the elne. All these were provided for him by his friends, and a pretty cassock put on upon him, upon the scaffold, wherein he was hanged. To be short, nothing was here deficient to honour his poor carcase, more beseeming a bridegroom than a criminal going to the gallows."—NICHOLL'S *Diary*.

> "*The grim Geneva ministers*
> *With anxious scowl drew near,*" p. 39.

The Presbyterian ministers beset Montrose both in prison and on the scaffold. The following extracts are from the diary of the Rev. Robert Traill, one of the persons who were appointed by the commission of the kirk "to deal with him:"—"By a warrant from the kirk, we staid a while with him about his soul's condition. But we found him continuing in his old pride, and taking very ill what was spoken to him, saying, 'I pray you, gentlemen, let me die in peace.' It was answered, that he might die in true peace, being reconciled to the Lord and to his kirk."—"We returned to the commission, and did show unto them what had passed among us. They, seeing that for the present he was not desiring relaxation from his censure of excommunication, did appoint Mr. Mungo Law and me to attend on the morrow on the scaffold, at the time of his execution, that, in case he should desire to be relaxed from his excommunication, we should be allowed to give it unto him in the name of the kirk, and to pray with him, and for him, *that what is loosed on earth might be loosed in heaven.*" But this pious intention, which may appear somewhat strange to the modern Calvinist, when the prevailing theories of the kirk regarding the efficacy of absolution are considered, was not destined to be fulfilled.   Mr. Traill goes on to say, "But he did not at all desire to be relaxed from his excommunication in the name of the kirk, *yea, did not look towards that place on the scaffold where we stood;* only he drew apart some of the magistrates, and spake a while with them, and then went up the ladder, in his red scarlet cassock, in a very stately manner."

> "*And he climbed the lofty ladder*
> *As it were the path to heaven*," p. 40.

"He was very earnest that he might have the liberty to keep on his hat; it was denied: he requested he might have the privilege to keep his cloak about him—neither could that be granted. Then, with a most undaunted courage, he went up to the top of that prodigious gibbet."—"The whole people gave a general groan; and it was very observable, that even those who, at his first appearance, had bitterly inveighed against him, could not now abstain from tears."—*Montrose Redivivus.*

THE HEART OF THE BRUCE.

HECTOR BOECE, in his very delightful, though somewhat apocryphal Chronicles of Scotland, tells us, that "quhen Schir James Dowglas was chosin as maist worthy of all Scotland to pass with King Robertis hart to the Holy Land, he put it in ane cais of gold, with arromitike and precious unyementis; and tuke with him Schir William Sinclare and Schir Robert Logan, with mony othir nobilmen, to the haly graif; quhare he buryit the said hart, with maist reverence and solempnitie that could be devisit."

But no contemporary historian bears out the statement of the old canon of Aberdeen. Froissart, Fordun, and Barbour all agree that the devotional pilgrimage of the Good Sir James was not destined to be accomplished, and that the heart of Scotland's greatest king and hero was brought back to the land of his nativity. Mr. Tytler, in few words, has so graphically recounted the leading events of this expedition, that I do not hesitate to adopt his narrative :—

"As soon as the season of the year permitted, Douglas, having the heart of his beloved master under his charge, set sail from Scotland, accompanied by a splendid retinue, and anchored off Sluys in Flanders, at this time the great seaport of the Netherlands. His object was to find out companions with whom he might travel to Jerusalem ; but he declined landing, and for twelve days received all visitors on board his ship with a state almost kingly.

47

"At Sluys he heard that Alonzo, the King of Leon and Castile, was carrying on war with Osmyn, the Moorish governor of Grenada. The religious mission which he had embraced, and the vows he had taken before leaving Scotland, induced Douglas to consider Alonzo's cause as a holy warfare; and, before proceeding to Jerusalem, he first determined to visit Spain, and to signalise his prowess against the Saracens. But his first field against the Infidels proved fatal to him who, in the long English war, had seen seventy battles. The circumstances of his death were striking and characteristic. In an action near Theba, on the borders of Andalusia, the Moorish cavalry were defeated; and, after their camp had been taken, Douglas, with his companions, engaged too eagerly in the pursuit, and, being separated from the main body of the Spanish army, a strong division of the Moors rallied and surrounded them. The Scottish knight endeavoured to cut his way through the Infidels, and in all probability would have succeeded, had he not again turned to rescue Sir William Saint Clair of Roslin, whom he saw in jeopardy. In attempting this, he was inextricably involved with the enemy. Taking from his neck the casket which contained the heart of Bruce, he cast it before him, and exclaimed with a loud voice, ' Now pass onward as thou wert wont, and Douglas will follow thee or die !' The action and the sentiment were heroic, and they were the last words and deed of a heroic life, for Douglas fell overpowered by his enemies; and three of his knights, and many of his companions, were slain along with their master. On the succeeding day, the body and the casket were both found on the field, and by his surviving friends conveyed to Scotland. The heart of Bruce was deposited at Melrose, and the body of the ' Good Sir James '—the name by which he is affectionately remembered by his countrymen—was consigned to the cemetery of his fathers in the parish church of Douglas."

A nobler death on the field of battle is not recorded in the annals of chivalry. In memory of this expedition, the Douglases have ever since carried the armorial bearings of the Bloody Heart surmounted by the Crown; and a similar distinction is borne by another family. Sir Simon of Lee, a distinguished companion of Douglas, was the person on whom, after the fall of his leader, the custody of the heart devolved. Hence the name of Lockhart, and their effigy, the Heart within a Fetterlock.

THE HEART OF THE BRUCE.

It was upon an April morn,
  While yet the frost lay hoar,
We heard Lord James's bugle-horn
  Sound by the rocky shore.

Then down we went, a hundred knights,
  All in our dark array,
And flung our armour in the ships
  That rode within the bay.

We spoke not as the shore grew less,
  But gazed in silence back,
Where the long billows swept away
  The foam behind our track.

And aye the purple hues decay'd
  Upon the fading hill,
And but one heart in all that ship
  Was tranquil, cold, and still.

The good Lord Douglas walk'd the deck,
  And oh, his brow was wan !
Unlike the flush it used to wear
  When in the battle van.—

"Come hither, come hither, my trusty knight,
  Sir Simon of the Lee ;
There is a freit lies near my soul
  I fain would tell to thee.

" Thou knowest the words King Robert spoke
 Upon his dying day,
How he bade me take his noble heart
 And carry it far away ;

" And lay it in the holy soil
 Where once the Saviour trod,
Since he might not bear the blessed Cross,
 Nor strike one blow for God.

" Last night as in my bed I lay,
 I dream'd a dreary dream :—
Methought I saw a Pilgrim stand
 In the moonlight's quivering beam.

" His robe was of the azure dye,
 Snow-white his scatter'd hairs,
And even such a cross he bore
 As good Saint Andrew bears.

" ' Why go you forth, Lord James,' he said,
 ' With spear and belted brand?
Why do you take its dearest pledge
 From this our Scottish land?

" ' The sultry breeze of Galilee
 Creeps through its groves of palm,
The olives on the Holy Mount
 Stand glittering in the calm.

" ' But 'tis not there that Scotland's heart
 Shall rest by God's decree,
Till the great angel calls the dead
 To rise from earth and sea !

" ' Lord James of Douglas, mark my rede !
 That heart shall pass once more
In fiery fight against the foe,
 As it was wont of yore.

" ' And it shall pass beneath the Cross,
   And save King Robert's vow,
But other hands shall bear it back,
   Not, James of Douglas, thou ! '

" Now, by thy knightly faith, I pray,
   Sir Simon of the Lee—
For truer friend had never man
   Than thou hast been to me—

" If ne'er upon the Holy Land
   'Tis mine in life to tread,
Bear thou to Scotland's kindly earth
   The relics of her dead."

The tear was in Sir Simon's eye
   As he wrung the warrior's hand—
" Betide me weal, betide me woe,
   I'll hold by thy command.

" But if in battle front, Lord James,
   'Tis ours once more to ride,
Nor force of man, nor craft of fiend,
   Shall cleave me from thy side ! "

And aye we sail'd, and aye we sail'd,
   Across the weary sea,
Until one morn the coast of Spain
   Rose grimly on our lee.

And as we rounded to the port,
   Beneath the watch-tower's wall,
We heard the clash of the atabals,
   And the trumpet's wavering call.

" 'Why sounds yon Eastern music here
   So wantonly and long,
And whose the crowd of armèd men
   That round yon standard throng ? "

"The Moors have come from Africa
  To spoil and waste and slay,
And King Alonzo of Castile
  Must fight with them to-day."

"Now shame it were," cried good Lord James,
  "Shall never be said of me,
That I and mine have turn'd aside,
  From the Cross in jeopardie!

"Have down, have down, my merry men all—
  Have down unto the plain;
We'll let the Scottish lion loose
  Within the fields of Spain!".

"Now welcome to me, noble lord,
  Thou and thy stalwart power;
Dear is the sight of a Christian knight
  Who comes in such an hour!

"Is it for bond or faith ye come,
  Or yet for golden fee?
Or bring ye France's lilies here,
  Or the flower of Burgundie?"

"God greet thee well, thou valiant King,
  Thee and thy belted peers—
Sir James of Douglas am I called,
  And these are Scottish spears.

"We do not fight for bond or plight,
  Nor yet for golden fee;
But for the sake of our blessed Lord,
  Who died upon the tree.

"We bring our great King Robert's heart
  Across the weltering wave,
To lay it in the holy soil
  Hard by the Saviour's grave.

"True pilgrims we, by land or sea,
   Where danger bars the way ;
And therefore are we here, Lord King,
   To ride with thee this day !"

The King has bent his stately head,
   And the tears were in his eyne—
"God's blessing on thee, noble knight,
   For this brave thought of thine !

"I know thy name full well, Lord James,
   And honour'd may I be,
That those who fought beside the Bruce
   Should fight this day for me !

"Take thou the leading of the van,
   And charge the Moors amain ;
There is not such a lance as thine
   In all the host of Spain !"

The Douglas turned towards us then,
   O but his glance was high !—
"There is not one of all my men
   But is as bold as I.

"There is not one of all my knights
   But bears as true a spear—
Then onwards ! Scottish gentlemen,
   And think—King Robert's here !"

The trumpets blew, the cross-bolts flew,
   The arrows flashed like flame,
As spur in side, and spear in rest,
   Against the foe we came.

And many a bearded Saracen
   Went down, both horse and man ;
For through their ranks we rode like corn,
   So furiously we ran !

But in behind our path they closed,
   Though fain to let us through,
For they were forty thousand men,
   And we were wondrous few.

We might not see a lance's length,
   So dense was their array,
But the long fell sweep of the Scottish blade
   Still held them hard at bay. .

" Make in ! make in !" Lord Douglas cried,
   " Make in, my brethren dear !
Sir William of Saint Clair is down ;
   We may not leave him here !

But thicker, thicker, grew the swarm,
   And sharper shot the rain,
And the horses reared amid the press,
   But they would not charge again.

" Now Jesu help thee," said Lord James,
   " Thou kind and true Saint Clair !
An' if I may not bring thee off,
   I'll die beside thee there ! "

Then in his stirrups up he stood,
   So lionlike and bold,
And held the precious heart aloft
   All in its case of gold.

He flung it from him, far ahead,
   And never spake he more,
But—" Pass thee first, thou dauntless heart,
   As thou wert wont of yore ! "

The roar of fight rose fiercer yet,
   And heavier still the stour,
Till the spears of Spain came shivering in,
   And swept away the Moor.

" Now praised be God, the day is won !
    They fly o'er flood and fell—
Why dost thou draw the rein so hard,
    Good knight, that fought so well ? "

"Oh, ride ye on, Lord King ! " he said,
    " And leave the dead to me,
For I must keep the dreariest watch
    That ever I shall dree !

" There lies, beside his master's heart,
    The Douglas, stark and grim ;
And woe is me I should be here,
    Not side by side with him !

" The world grows cold, my arm is old,
    And thin my lyart hair,
And all that I loved best on earth
    Is stretch'd before me there.

" O Bothwell banks ! that bloom so bright,
    Beneath the sun of May,
The heaviest cloud that ever blew
    Is bound for you this day.

" And, Scotland, thou may'st veil thy head
    In sorrow and in pain ;
The sorest stroke upon thy brow
    Hath fallen this day in Spain !

" We'll bear them back unto our ship,
    We'll bear them o'er the sea,
And lay them in the hallowed earth,
    Within our own countrie.

" And be thou strong of heart, Lord King,
    For this I tell thee sure,
The sod that drank the Douglas' blood
    Shall never bear the Moor ! "

The King he lighted from his horse,
   He flung his brand away,
And took the Douglas by the hand,
   So stately as he lay.

"God give thee rest, thou valiant soul,
   That fought so well for Spain ;
I'd rather half my land were gone,
   So thou wert here again !"

We bore the good Lord James away,
   And the priceless heart he bore,
And heavily we steered our ship
   Towards the Scottish shore.

No welcome greeted our return,
   Nor clang of martial tread,
But all were dumb and hushed as death
   Before the mighty dead.

We laid our chief in Douglas Kirk,
   The heart in fair Melrose ;
And woeful men were we that day—
   God grant their souls repose !

The Burial March of Dundee.

—⌇⋙⋘⌇—

IT is very much to be regretted that no competent
person has as yet undertaken the task of compiling
a full and authentic biography of Lord Viscount
Dundee. His memory has consequently been left
at the mercy of misrepresentation and malignity ;
and the pen of romance has been freely employed
to portray as a bloody assassin one of the most
accomplished men and gallant soldiers of his age.
It was the misfortune of Claverhouse to have
lived in so troublous an age and country. The
religious differences of Scotland were then at their
greatest height, and there is hardly any act of
atrocity and rebellion which had not been committed by the insurgents. The royal authority was
openly and publicly disowned in the western districts : the Archbishop of St. Andrews, after more
than one hairbreadth escape, was waylaid, and bar-
barously murdered by an armed gang of fanatics
on Magus Muir ; and his daughter was wounded
and maltreated while interceding for the old man's
life. The country was infested by banditti, who
took every possible opportunity of shooting down
and massacring any of the straggling soldiery ; the
clergy were attacked and driven from their houses ;
so that, throughout a considerable portion of Scotland, there was no security either for property or
for life. It is now the fashion to praise and mag-
nify the Covenanters as the most innocent and
persecuted of men ; but those who are so ready
with their sympathy, rarely take the pains to satisfy

themselves, by reference to the annals of the time, of the true character of those men whom they blindly venerate as martyrs. They forget, in their zeal for religious freedom, that even the purest and holiest of causes may be sullied and disgraced by the deeds of its upholders, and that a wild and frantic profession of faith is not always a test of genuine piety. It is not in the slightest degree necessary to discuss whether the royal prerogative was at that time arbitrarily used, or whether the religious freedom of the nation was unduly curtailed. Both points may be, and indeed are, admitted,—for it is impossible to vindicate the policy of the measures adopted by the two last monarchs of the house of Stuart; but neither admission will clear the Covenanters from the stain of deliberate cruelty.

After the battle of Philiphaugh, the royalist prisoners were butchered in cold blood, under the superintendence of a clerical emissary, who stood by rubbing his hands, and exclaiming— "The wark gangs bonnily on!" Were I to transcribe from the pamphlets before me the list of the murders which were perpetrated by the country people on the soldiery, officers, and gentlemen of loyal principles, during the reign of Charles II., I believe that no candid person would be surprised at the severe retaliation which was made. It must be remembered that the country was then under military law, and that the strongest orders had been issued ‚by the Government to the officers in command of the troops, to use every means in their power for the effectual repression of the disturbances. The necessity of such orders will become apparent, when we reflect that, besides the open actions at Aird's Moss and Drumclog, the city of Glasgow was attacked, and the royal forces compelled for a time to fall back upon Stirling.

Under such circumstances it is no wonder if the soldiery were severe in their reprisals. Innocent blood may no doubt have been shed, and in some cases even wantonly ; for when rebellion has grown into civil war, and the ordinary course of the law is put in abeyance, it is always impossible to restrain military license. But it is most unfair to lay the whole odium of such acts upon those who were in command, and to dishonour the fair name of gentlemen, by attributing to them personally the commission of deeds of which they were absolutely ignorant. To this day the peasantry of the western districts of Scotland entertain the idea that Claverhouse was a sort of fiend in human shape, tall, muscular, and hideous in aspect, secured by infernal spells from the chance of perishing by any ordinary weapon, and mounted upon a huge black horse, the especial gift of Beelzebub ! On this charger it is supposed that he could ride up precipices as easily as he could traverse the level ground—that he was constantly accompanied by a body of desperadoes, vulgarly known by such euphonious titles as " Hell's Tam," and "the De'il's Jock," and that his whole time was occupied, day and night, in hunting Covenanters upon the hills ! Almost every rebel who was taken in arms and shot, is supposed to have met his death from the individual pistol of Claverhouse ; and the tales which, from time to time, have been written by such ingenious persons as the late Mr. Galt and the Ettrick Shepherd, have quietly been assumed as facts, and added to the store of our traditionary knowledge. It is in vain to hint that the chief commanders of the forces in Scotland could have found little leisure, even had they possessed the taste, for pursuing single insurgents. Such suggestions are an insult to martyrology ; and many a parish of the west would be indignant were it averred that the tenant of its gray stone had suffered by a meaner hand.

When we look at the portrait of Claverhouse, and survey the calm, melancholy, and beautiful features of the devoted soldier, it appears almost incredible that he should ever have suffered under such an overwhelming load of misrepresentation. But when—discarding modern historians, who in too many instances do not seem to entertain the slightest scruple in dealing with the memory of the dead—we turn to the writings of his contemporaries who knew the man, his character appears in a very different light. They describe him as one who was stainless in his honour, pure in his faith, wise in council, resolute in action, and utterly free from that selfishness which disgraced the Scottish statesmen of the time. No one dares question his loyalty, for he sealed that confession with his blood; and it is universally admitted, that with him fell the last hopes of the reinstatement of the house of Stuart.

I may perhaps be permitted here, in the absence of a better chronicler, to mention a few particulars of his life, which, I believe, are comparatively unknown. John Graham of Claverhouse was a cadet of the family of Fintrie, connected by intermarriage with the blood-royal of Scotland. After completing his studies at the University of St. Andrews, he entered, as was the national custom for gentlemen of good birth and limited means, into foreign service, served some time in France as a volunteer, and afterwards went to Holland. He very soon received a commission, as a cornet in a regiment of horse-guards, from the Prince of Orange, nephew of Charles II. and James VII., and who afterwards married the Princess Mary. His manner at that time is thus described :—" He was then ane esquire, under the title of John Graham of Claverhouse; but the vivacity of his parts, and the delicacy and justice of his understanding and judgment, joyned with a certain vigour of mind and activity of body, distinguished him in such a manner from all others of his rank, that though he lived in a superior character, yet he acquired the love and esteem of all his equals, as well as of those who had the advantage of him in dignity and estate."

By one of those singular accidents which we
occasionally meet with in history, Graham, afterwards destined to become his most formidable
opponent, saved the life of the Prince of Orange
at the battle of St. Neff. The Prince's horse had
been killed, and he himself was in the grasp of the
enemy, when the young cornet rode to his rescue,
freed him from his assailants, and mounted him
on his own steed. For this service he received a
captain's commission, and the promise of the first
regiment that should fall vacant.

But even in early life William of Orange was
not famous for keeping his promises. Some years
afterwards, a vacancy in one of the Scottish
regiments in the Prince's service occurred, and
Claverhouse, relying upon the previous assurance,
preferred his claim. It was disregarded, and Mr.
Collier, afterwards Earl of Portmore, was appointed
over his head. It would seem that Graham had
suspected some foul play on the part of this
gentleman, for, shortly after, they accidentally
met and had an angry altercation. This circumstance having come to the ears of the Prince, he
sent for Captain Graham, and administered a
sharp rebuke. I give the remainder of this incident in the words of the old writer, because it
must be considered a very remarkable one, as
illustrating the fiery spirit and dauntless independence of Claverhouse.

"The Captain answered, that he was indeed
in the wrong, since it was more his Highness's
business to have resented that quarrel than his;
because Mr. Collier had less injured him in
disappointing him of the regiment, than he had
done his Highness in making him break his word.
'Then,' replied the Prince in an angry tone, 'I
make you full reparation, for I bestow on you
what is more valuable than a regiment when I
give you your right arm!' The Captain sub-
joined, that since his Highness had the goodness
to give him his liberty, he resolved to employ

himself elsewhere, for he would not longer serve a Prince that had broken his word.

"The Captain, having thus thrown up his commission, was preparing in haste for his voyage, when a messenger arrived from the Prince, with two hundred guineas for the horse on which he had saved his life. The Captain sent the horse, but ordered the gold to be distributed among the grooms of the Prince's stables. It is said, however, that his Highness had the generosity to write to the King and the Duke, recommending him as a fine gentleman and a brave officer, fit for any office, civil or military."

On his arrival in Britain he was well received by the court, and immediately appointed to a high military command in Scotland. It would be beyond the scope of the present paper to enter minutely into the details of his service during the stormy period when Scotland was certainly misgoverned, and when there was little unity, but much disorder in the land. In whatever point of view we regard the history of those times, the aspect is a mournful one indeed. Church and State never was a popular cry in Scotland; and the peculiar religious tendencies which had been exhibited by a large portion of the nation, at the time of the Reformation, rendered the return of tranquillity hopeless, until the hierarchy was displaced, and a humbler form of Church government, more suited to the feelings of the people, substituted in its stead.

Three years after the accession of James VII., Claverhouse was raised to the peerage, by the title of Lord Viscount Dundee. He was major-general, and second in command of the royal forces, when the Prince of Orange landed, and earnestly entreated King James to be allowed to march against him, offering to stake his head on the successful result of the enterprise. There is little doubt, from the great popularity of Lord Dundee with the army, that, had such consent been given, William would

have found more than a match in his old officer;
but the King seemed absolutely infatuated, and
refused to allow a drop of blood to be shed in his
quarrel, though the great bulk of the population of
England were clearly and enthusiastically in his
favour. One of the most gifted of our modern
poets, the Honourable George Sydney Smythe, has
beautifully illustrated this event.

" Then out spake gallant Claverhouse, and his soul
    thrilled wild and high,
And he showed the King his subjects, and he prayed him
    not to fly.
O never yet was captain so dauntless as Dundee—
He has sworn to chase the Hollander back to his Zuyder-
    Zee !"

But though James quitted his kingdom, the stern
loyalty of Dundee was nothing moved. Alone
and without escort he traversed England, and presented himself at the Convention of Estates, then
assembled at Edinburgh for the purpose of re-
ceiving the message from the Prince of Orange.
The meeting was a very strange one. Many of the
nobility and former members of the Scottish Parliament absolutely declined attending it,—some on
the ground that it was not a legal assembly, having
been summoned by the Prince of Orange, and
others because, in such a total disruption of order,
they judged it safest to abstain from taking any
prominent part. This gave an immense ascendency
to the Revolution party, who further proceeded to
strengthen their position by inviting to Edinburgh
large bodies of the armed population of the west.
After defending for several days the cause of his
master with as much eloquence as vigour, Dundee,
finding that the majority of the Convention were
resolved to offer the crown of Scotland to the
Prince, and having, moreover, received sure information that some of the wild fanatic Whigs, with
Daniel Ker of Kersland at their head, had formed
a plot for his assassination, quitted Edinburgh with

about fifty horsemen, and, after a short interview
—celebrated by Sir Walter Scott in one of his
grandest ballads—with the Duke of Gordon at the
Castle rock, directed his steps towards the north.
After a short stay at his house of Duddope, during
which he received, by order of the Council, who
were thoroughly alarmed at his absence, a summons
through a Lyon herald to return to Edinburgh
under pain of high treason, he passed into the
Gordon country, where he was joined by the Earl
of Dunfermline with a small party of about sixty
horse.   His retreat was timeous, for General
Mackay, who commanded for the Prince of Orange,
had despatched a strong force, with instructions to
make him prisoner.   From this time, until the day
of his death, he allowed himself no repose.   Imi-
tating the example, and inheriting the enthusiasm
of his great predecessor Montrose, he invoked the
loyalty of the clans to assist him in the struggle for
legitimacy,—and he did not appeal to them in vain.
His name was a spell to rouse the ardent spirits of
the mountaineers ; and not the Great Marquis
himself, in the height of his renown, was more
sincerely welcomed and more fondly loved than
" Ian dhu nan Cath,"—Dark John of the Battles,
—the name by which Lord Dundee is still remembered in Highland song.   In the meantime the
Convention, terrified at their danger, and dreading
a Highland inroad, had despatched Mackay, a
military officer of great experience, with a considerable body of troops, to quell the threatened
insurrection.   He was encountered by Dundee,
and compelled to evacuate the high country and
fall back upon the Lowlands, where he subsequently
received reinforcements, and again marched north-
ward.   The Highland host was assembled at Blair,
though not in great force, when the news of
Mackay's advance arrived ; and a council of the
chiefs and officers was summoned, to determine
whether it would be most advisable to fall back
upon the glens and wild fastnesses of the High-

lands, or to meet the enemy at once, though with a force far inferior to his.

Most of the old officers, who had been trained in the foreign wars, were of the former opinion—"alleging that it was neither prudent nor cautious to risk an engagement against an army of disciplined men, that exceeded theirs in number by more than a half." But both Glengarry and Locheill, to the great satisfaction of the General, maintained the contrary view, and argued that neither hunger nor fatigue were so likely to depress the Highlanders, as a retreat when the enemy was in view. The account of the discussion is so interesting, and so characteristic of Dundee, that I shall take leave to quote its termination in the words of Drummond of Balhaldy :—

"An advice so hardy and resolute could not miss to please the generous Dundee. His looks seemed to heighten with an air of delight and satisfaction all the while Locheill was speaking. He told his council that they had heard his sentiments from the mouth of a person who had formed his judgment upon infallible proofs drawn from a long experience, and an intimate acquaintance with the persons and subject he spoke of. Not one in the company offering to contradict their general, it was unanimously agreed to fight.

"When the news of this vigorous resolution spread through the army, nothing was heard but acclamations of joy, which exceedingly pleased their gallant general ; but before the council broke up, Locheill begged to be heard for a few words. 'My Lord,' said he, 'I have just now declared, in presence of this honourable company, that I was resolved to give an implicit obedience to all your Lordship s commands ; but I humbly beg leave, in name of these gentlemen, to give the word of command for this one time. It is the voice of your council, and their orders are, that you do not engage personally. Your Lordship's business is to have an eye on all parts, and to issue out your commands as you shall think proper; it is ours to execute them with promptitude and courage. On your Lordship depends the fate, not only of this little brave army, but also of our king and country. If your Lordship deny us this reasonable demand, for my own part I declare, that neither I, nor any I am concerned in, shall draw a sword on this important occasion, whatever construction shall be put upon the matter.'

" Locheill was seconded in this by the whole council; but Dundee begged leave to be heard in his turn. 'Gentlemen,' said he, 'as I am absolutely convinced, and have had repeated proofs, of your zeal for the king's service, and of your affection to me as his General and your friend, so I am fully sensible that my engaging personally this day may be of some loss if I shall chance to be killed. But I beg leave of you, however, to allow me to give one *shear-darg* (that is, one harvest-day's work) to the king, my master, that I may have an opportunity of convincing the brave clans, that I can hazard my life in that service as freely as the meanest of them. Ye know their temper, gentlemen; and if they do not think I have personal courage enough, they will not esteem me hereafter, nor obey my commands with cheerfulness. Allow me this single favour, and I here promise, upon my honour, never again to risk my person while I have that of commanding you.'

" The council, finding him inflexible, broke up, and the army marched directly towards the Pass of Killiecrankie."

Those who have visited that romantic spot need not be reminded of its peculiar features, for these, once seen, must dwell for ever in the memory. The lower part of the Pass is a stupendous mountain-chasm, scooped out by the waters of the Garry, which here descend in a succession of roaring cataracts and pools. The old road, which ran almost parallel to the river and close upon its edge, was extremely narrow, and wound its way beneath a wall of enormous crags, surmounted by a natural forest of birch, oak, and pine. An army cooped up in that gloomy ravine would have as little chance of escape from the onset of an enterprising partisan corps, as had the Bavarian troops when attacked by the Tyrolese in the steep defiles of the Inn. General Mackay, however, had made his arrangements with consummate tact and skill, and had calculated his time so well, that he was enabled to clear the Pass before the Highlanders could reach it from the other side. Advancing upwards, the passage becomes gradually broader, until, just below the House of Urrard, there is a considerable width of meadow-land. It was here that Mackay took up his position, and arrayed his troops, on observing that the heights above were occupied by the army of Dundee.

The forces of the latter scarcely amounted to one-third of those of his antagonist, which were drawn up in line without any reserve. He was therefore compelled, in making his dispositions, to leave considerable gaps in his own line, which gave Mackay a further advantage. The right of Dundee's army was formed of the M'Lean, Glengarry, and Clanranald regiments, along with some Irish levies. In the centre was Dundee himself, at the head of a small and ill-equipped body of cavalry, composed of Lowland gentlemen and their followers, and about forty of his old troopers. The Camerons and Skyemen, under the command of Locheill and Sir Donald Macdonald of Sleat, were stationed on the left. During the time occupied by these dispositions, a brisk cannonade was opened by Mackay's artillery, which materially increased the impatience of the Highlanders to come to close quarters. At last the word was given to advance, and the whole line rushed forward with the terrific impetuosity peculiar to a charge of the clans. They received the fire of the regular troops without flinching, reserved their own until they were close at hand, poured in a murderous volley, and then, throwing away their firelocks, attacked the enemy with the broadsword.

The victory was almost instantaneous, but it was bought at a terrible price. Through some mistake or misunderstanding, a portion of the cavalry, instead of following their general, who had charged directly for the guns, executed a manœuvre which threw them into disorder ; and, when last seen in the battle, Dundee, accompanied only by the Earl of Dunfermline and about sixteen gentlemen, was entering into the cloud of smoke, standing up in his stirrups, and waving to the others to come on. It was in this attitude that he appears to have received his death-wound. On returning from the pursuit, the Highlanders found him dying on the field.

It would be difficult to point out another instance in which the maintenance of a great cause depended solely upon the life of a single man. Whilst Dundee survived, Scotland at least was not lost to the Stuarts, for, shortly before the battle, he had received assurance that the greater part of the organised troops in the north were devoted to his person, and ready to join him ; and the victory of Killiecrankie would have been followed by a general rising of the loyal gentlemen in the Lowlands. But with his fall the enterprise was over.

I hope I shall not be accused of exaggerating the importance of this battle, which, according to the writer I have already quoted, was best proved by the consternation into which the opposite party were thrown at the first news of Mackay's defeat. "The Duke of Hamilton, commissioner for the parliament which then sat at Edinburgh, and the rest of the ministry, were struck with such a panic, that some of them were for retiring into England, others into the western shires of Scotland, where all the people, almost to a man, befriended them ; nor knew they whether to abandon the government, or to stay a few days until they saw what use my

Lord Dundee would make of his victory. They knew the rapidity of his motions, and were convinced that he would allow them no time to deliberate. On this account it was debated, whether such of the nobility and gentry as were confined for adhering to their old master, should be immediately set at liberty or more closely shut up; and though the last was determined on, yet the greatest revolutionists among them made private and frequent visits to these prisoners, excusing what was past, from a fatal necessity of the times, which obliged them to give a seeming compliance, but protesting that they always wished well to King James, as they should soon have occasion to show when my Lord Dundee advanced."

" The next morning after the battle," says Drummond, "the Highland army had more the air of the shattered remains of broken troops than of conquerors; for here it was literally true that

'The vanquished triumphed, and the victors mourned.'

The death of their brave general, and the loss of so many of their friends, were inexhaustible fountains of grief and sorrow. They closed the last scene of this mournful tragedy in obsequies of their lamented general, and of the other gentlemen who fell with him, and interred them in the church of Blair of Atholl with a real funeral solemnity, there not being present one single person who did not participate in the general affliction."

I close this notice of a great soldier and devoted loyalist, by transcribing the beautiful epitaph composed by Dr. Pitcairn :—

> "Ultime Scotorum ! potuit, quo sospite solo,
>   Libertas patriæ salva fuisse tuæ :
> Te moriente, novos accepit Scotia cives,
>   Accepitque novos, te moriente, deos.
> Illa nequit superesse tibi, tu non potes illi,
>   Ergo Caledoniæ nomen inane, vale.
> Tuque vale, gentis priscæ fortissime ductor,
>   Ultime Scotorum, ac ultime Grame, vale !"

THE BURIAL MARCH OF DUNDEE.

SOUND the fife, and cry the slogan—
  Let the pibroch shake the air
With its wild triumphal music,
  Worthy of the freight we bear.
Let the ancient hills of Scotland
  Hear once more the battle-song
Swell within their glens and valleys
  As the clansmen march along !
Never from the field of combat,
  Never from the deadly fray,
Was a nobler trophy carried
  Than we bring with us to-day ;
Never, since the valiant Douglas
  On his dauntless bosom bore
Good King Robert's heart—the priceless—
  To our dear Redeemer's shore !
Lo ! we bring with us the hero—
  Lo ! we bring the conquering Græme,
Crowned as best beseems a victor
  From the altar of his fame ;
Fresh and bleeding from the battle
  Whence his spirit took its flight,
Midst the crashing charge of squadrons,
  And the thunder of the fight !
Strike, I say, the notes of triumph,
  As we march o'er moor and lea !
Is there any here will venture
  To bewail our dead Dundee ?
Let the widows of the traitors
  Weep until their eyes are dim !
Wail ye may full well for Scotland—
  Let none dare to mourn for him !

See! above his glorious body
  Lies the royal banner's fold—
See! his valiant blood is mingled
  With its crimson and its gold.
See how calm he looks and stately,
  Like a warrior on his shield,
Waiting till the flush of morning
  Breaks along the battle-field!
See—Oh never more, my comrades!
  Shall we see that falcon eye
Redden with its inward lightning,
  As the hour of fight drew nigh;
Never shall we hear the voice that,
  Clearer than the trumpet's call,
Bade us strike for King and Country,
  Bade us win the field or fall!

On the heights of Killiecrankie
  Yester-morn our army lay:
Slowly rose the mist in columns
  From the river's broken way;
Hoarsely roared the swollen torrent,
  And the pass was wrapped in gloom,
When the clansmen rose together
  From their lair amidst the broom.
Then we belted on our tartans,
  And our bonnets down we drew,
And we felt our broadswords' edges,
  And we proved them to be true;
And we prayed the prayer of soldiers,
  And we cried the gathering-cry,
And we clasped the hands of kinsmen,
  And we swore to do or die!
Then our leader rode before us
  On his war-horse black as night—
Well the Cameronian rebels
  Knew that charger in the fight!—
And a cry of exultation
  From the bearded warriors rose;
For we loved the house of Claver'se,
  And we thought of good Montrose.

D

But he raised his hand for silence—
  "Soldiers! I have sworn a vow:
Ere the evening-star shall glisten
  On Schehallion's lofty brow,
Either we shall rest in triumph,
  Or another of the Græmes
Shall have died in battle-harness
  For his Country and King James!
Think upon the Royal Martyr—
  Think of what his race endure—
Think on him whom butchers murder'd
  On the field of Magus Muir :—
By his sacred blood I charge ye,
  By the ruin'd hearth and shrine—
By the blighted hopes of Scotland,
  By your injuries and mine—
Strike this day as if the anvil
  Lay beneath your blows the while,
Be they Covenanting traitors,
  Or the brood of false Argyle!
Strike! and drive the trembling rebels
  Backwards o'er the stormy Forth;
Let them tell their pale Convention
  How they fared within the North.
Let them tell that Highland honour
  Is not to be bought nor sold,
That we scorn their Prince's anger,
  As we loathe his foreign gold.
Strike! and when the fight is over,
  If ye look in vain for me,
Where the dead are lying thickest,
  Search for him that was Dundee!"

Loudly then the hills re-echoed
  With our answer to his call,
But a deeper echo sounded
  In the bosoms of us all.
For the lands of wide Breadalbane,
  Not a man who heard him speak
Would that day have left the battle.
  Burning eye and flushing cheek

Told the clansmen's fierce emotion,
    And they harder drew their breath;
For their souls were strong within them,
    Stronger than the grasp of death.
Soon we heard a challenge-trumpet
    Sounding in the pass below,
And the distant tramp of horses,
    And the voices of the foe:
Down we crouched amid the bracken,
    Till the Lowland ranks drew near,
Panting like the hounds in summer,
    When they scent the stately deer.
From the dark defile emerging,
    Next we saw the squadrons come,
Leslie's foot and Leven's troopers
    Marching to the tuck of drum;
Through the scattered wood of birches,
    O'er the broken ground and heath,
Wound the long battalion slowly,
    Till they gained the field beneath;
Then we bounded from our covert.—
    Judge how looked the Saxons then,
When they saw the rugged mountain
    Start to life with armèd men!
Like a tempest down the ridges
    Swept the hurricane of steel,
Rose the slogan of Macdonald—
    Flashed the broadsword of Locheill!
Vainly sped the withering volley
    'Mongst the foremost of our band-
On we poured until we met them,
    Foot to foot, and hand to hand.
Horse and man went down like drift-wood
    When the floods are black at Yule,
And their carcasses are whirling
    In the Garry's deepest pool.
Horse and man went down before us—
    Living foe there tarried none
On the field of Killicrankie,
    When that stubborn fight was done!

And the evening-star was shining
  On Schehallion's distant head,
When we wiped our bloody broadswords,
  And returned to count the dead.
There we found him, gashed and gory,
  Stretch'd upon the cumbered plain,
As he told us where to seek him,
  In the thickest of the slain.
And a smile was on his visage,
  For within his dying ear
Pealed the joyful note of triumph,
  And the clansmen's clamorous cheer :
So, amidst the battle's thunder,
  Shot, and steel, and scorching flame,
In the glory of his manhood
  Passed the spirit of the Græme !

Open wide the vaults of Athol,
  Where the bones of heroes rest—
Open wide the hallowed portals
  To receive another guest !
Last of Scots, and last of freemen—
  Last of all that dauntless race
Who would rather die unsullied
  Than outlive the land's disgrace !
O thou lion-hearted warrior !
  Reck not of the after-time :
Honour may be deemed dishonour,
  Loyalty be called a crime.
Sleep in peace with kindred ashes
  Of the noble and the true,
Hands that never failed their country,
  Hearts that never baseness knew.
Sleep !—and till the latest trumpet
  Wakes the dead from earth and sea,
Scotland shall not boast a braver
  Chieftain than our own Dundee !

THE WIDOW OF GLENCOE.

THE Massacre of Glencoe is an event which neither can nor ought to be forgotten. It was a deed of the worst treason and cruelty—a barbarous infraction of all laws, human and divine; and it exhibits in their foulest perfidy the true characters of the authors and abettors of the Revolution.

After the battle of Killiecrankie the cause of the Scottish royalists declined, rather from the want of a competent leader than from any disinclination on the part of a large section of the nobility and gentry to vindicate the right of King James. No person of adequate talents or authority was found to supply the place of the great and gallant Lord Dundee; for General Cannon, who succeeded in command, was not only deficient in military skill, but did not possess the confidence, nor understand the character of the Highland chiefs, who, with their clansmen, constituted by far the most important section of the army. Accordingly no enterprise of any importance was attempted; and the disastrous issue of the Battle of the Boyne led to a negotiation which terminated in the entire disbanding of the royal forces. By this treaty, which was expressly sanctioned by William of Orange, a full and unreserved indemnity and pardon was granted to all of the Highlanders who had taken arms, with a proviso that they should first subscribe the oath of allegiance to William and Mary, before the 1st of January 1692, in presence of the Lords of the Scottish Council, "or of the Sheriffs or their deputies of the respective shires wherein they lived." The letter of William addressed to the Privy Council, and ordering proclamation to be made to the above effect, contained also the following significant passage:—"That ye communicate our pleasure to the Governor of Inverlochy, and other commanders, that they be exact and diligent in their several posts; but that they show no more zeal against the Highlanders after their submission, *than they have ever done formerly when these were in open rebellion.*"

This enigmatical sentence, which in reality was intended, as the sequel will show, to be interpreted in the most cruel manner, appears to have caused some perplexity in the Council, as that body deemed it necessary to apply for more distinct and specific instructions, which, however, were not then issued. It had been especially stipulated by the chiefs, as an indispensable preliminary to their treaty, that they should have leave to communicate with King James, then residing at St. Germains, for the purpose of obtaining his permission and warrant previous to submitting themselves to the existing government. That article had been sanctioned by William before the proclamation was issued, and a special messenger was despatched to France for that purpose.

In the meantime, troops were gradually and cautiously advanced to the confines of the Highlands, and, in some instances, actually quartered on the inhabitants. The condition of the country was perfectly tranquil. No disturbances whatever occurred in the north or west of Scotland; Locheill and the other chiefs were awaiting the communication from St. Germains, and held themselves bound in honour to remain inactive; whilst the remainder of the royalist forces (for whom separate terms had been made) were left unmolested at Dunkeld.

But rumours, which are too clearly traceable to the emissaries of the new government, asserting the preparation made for an immediate landing of King James at the head of a large body of the French, were industriously circulated, and by many were implicitly believed. The infamous policy which dictated such a course is now apparent. The term of the amnesty or truce granted by the proclamation expired with the year 1691, and all who had not taken the oath of allegiance before that term, were to be proceeded against with the utmost severity. The proclamation was issued upon the 29th of August : consequently, only four months were allowed for the complete submission of the Highlands.

Not one of the chiefs subscribed until the mandate from King James arrived. That document, which is dated from St. Germains on the 12th of December 1691, reached Dunkeld eleven days afterwards, and, consequently, but a very short time before the indemnity expired. The bearer, Major Menzies, was so fatigued that he could proceed no farther on his journey, but forwarded the mandate by an express to the commander of the royal forces, who was then at Glengarry. It was therefore impossible that the document could be circulated through the Highlands within the prescribed period. Locheill, says Drummond of Balhaldy, did not receive his copy till about thirty hours before the time was out, and appeared before the sheriff at Inverara, where he took the oaths upon the very day on which the indemnity expired.

That a general massacre throughout the Highlands was contemplated by the Whig government, is a fact established by overwhelming evidence. In the course of the subsequent investigation before the Scots Parliament, letters were produced from Sir John Dalrymple, then Master of Stair, one of the secretaries of state in attendance upon the court, which too clearly indicate the intentions of William. In one of these, dated 1st December 1694—*a month*, be it observed, before the amnesty expired — and addressed to Lieutenant-Colonel Hamilton, there are the following words :—" The winter is the only season in which we are sure the Highlanders cannot escape us, *nor carry their wives, bairns,* and cattle to the mountains." And in another letter, written only two days afterwards, he says,—"It is the only time that they cannot escape you, for human constitution cannot endure to be long out of houses. *This is the proper season to maule them in the cold long nights."* And in January thereafter, he informed Sir Thomas Livingston that the design was "to destroy entirely the country of Lochaber, Locheill's lands, Keppoch's, Glengarry's, Appin, and Glencoe. I assure you," he continues, "your power shall be full enough, *and I hope the soldiers will not trouble the Government with prisoners."*

Locheill was more fortunate than others of his friends and neighbours. According to Drummond, —"Major Menzies, who, upon his arrival, had observed the whole forces of the kingdom ready to invade the Highlands, as he wrote to General Buchan, foreseeing the unhappy consequences, not only begged that general to send expresses to all parts with orders immediately to submit, but also wrote to Sir Thomas Livingston, praying him to supplicate the Council for a prorogation of the time, in regard that he was so excessively fatigued, that he was obliged to stop some days to repose a little; and that though he should send expresses, yet it was impossible they could reach the distant parts in such time as to allow the several persons concerned the benefit of the indemnity within the space limited; besides, that some persons having put the Highlanders in a bad temper, he was confident to persuade them to submit, if a further time were allowed. Sir Thomas presented this letter to the Council on the 5th of January 1692, but they refused to give any answer, and ordered him to transmit the same to Court."

The reply of William of Orange was a letter, countersigned by Dalrymple, in which upon the

recital that "several of the chieftains and many
of their clans have not taken the benefit of our
gracious indemnity," he gave orders for a general
massacre. "To that end, we have given Sir
Thomas Livingston orders to employ our troops
(which we have already conveniently posted) to
cut off these obstinate rebels *by all manner of hos-
tility;* and we do require you to give him your
assistance and concurrence in all other things that
may conduce to that service; and because these
rebels, to avoid our forces, may draw themselves,
their families, goods, or cattle, to lurk or be concealed among their neighbours: therefore, we
require and authorise you to emit a proclamation
to be published at the market-crosses of these or
the adjacent shires where the rebels reside, dis-
charging upon the highest penalties the law allows,
any reset, correspondence, or intercommuning with
these rebels." This monstrous mandate, which
was in fact the death-warrant of many thousand
innocent people, no distinction being made of age
or sex, would, in all human probability, have been
put into execution, but for the remonstrance of one
high-minded nobleman. Lord Carmarthen, afterwards Duke of Leeds, accidentally became aware
of the proposed massacre, and personally remon-
strated with the monarch against a measure which
he denounced as at once cruel and impolitic.
After much discussion, William, influenced rather
by an apprehension that so savage and sweeping
an act might prove fatal to his new authority,
than by any compunction or impulse of humanity,
agreed to recall the general order, and to limit
himself, in the first instance, to a single deed of
butchery, by way of testing the temper of the
nation. Some difficulty seems to have arisen in
the selection of the fittest victim. Both Keppoch
and Glencoe were named, but the personal rancour of Secretary Dalrymple decided the doom of
the latter. The secretary wrote thus:—"Argyle
tells me that Glencoe hath not taken the oath,

at which I rejoice. It is a great work of charity to be exact in rooting out that damnable set." The final instructions regarding Glencoe, which were issued on 16th January 1692, are as follows :—

"WILLIAM R.—As for M'Ian of Glencoe and that tribe, if they can be well distinguished from the rest of the Highlanders, it will be proper for public justice to extirpate that set of thieves.   W. R."

This letter is remarkable as being signed and countersigned by William alone, contrary to the usual practice. The Secretary was no doubt desirous to screen himself from after responsibility, and was further aware that the royal signature would ensure a rigorous execution of the sentence.

Macdonald, or, as he was more commonly designed, M'Ian of Glencoe, was the head of a considerable sept or branch of the great Clan-Coila, and was lineally descended from the ancient Lords of the Isles, and from the royal family of Scotland—the common ancestor of the Macdonalds having espoused a daughter of Robert II. He was, according to a contemporary testimony, "a person of great integrity, honour, good nature, and courage ; and his loyalty to his old master, King James, was such, that he continued in arms from Dundee's first appearing in the Highlands, till the fatal treaty that brought on his ruin." In common with the other chiefs, he had omitted taking the benefit of the indemnity until he received the sanction of King James : but the copy of that document which was forwarded to him, unfortunately arrived too late. The weather was so excessively stormy at the time that there was no possibility of penetrating from Glencoe to Inverara, the place where the sheriff resided, before the expiry of the stated period ; and M'Ian accordingly adopted the only practicable mode of signifying his submission, by making his way with great difficulty to Fort-William, then called

Inverlochy, and tendering his signature to the military Governor there. That officer was not authorised to receive it, but at the earnest entreaty of the chief, he gave him a certificate of his appearance and tender, and on New Year's Day, 1692, M'Ian reached Inverara, where he produced that paper as evidence of his intentions, and prevailed upon the sheriff, Sir James Campbell of Ardkinglass, to administer the oaths required. After that ceremony, which was immediately intimated to the Privy Council, had been performed, the unfortunate gentleman returned home, in the full conviction that he had thereby made peace with government for himself and for his clan. But his doom was already sealed.

A company of the Earl of Argyle's regiment had been previously quartered in Glencoe. These men, though Campbells, and hereditarily obnoxious to the Macdonalds, Camerons, and other of the loyal clans, were yet countrymen, and were kindly and hospitably received. Their captain, Robert Campbell of Glenlyon, was connected with the family of Glencoe through the marriage of a niece, and was resident under the roof of the chief. And yet this was the very troop selected for the horrid service.

Special instructions were sent to the major of the regiment, one Duncanson, then quartered at Ballachulish—a morose, brutal, and savage man—who accordingly wrote to Campbell of Glenlyon in the following terms :—

"BALLACHOLIS, 12 *February* 1692.

"SIR,—You are hereby ordered to fall upon the rebels, the M'Donalds of Glencoe, and putt all to the sword under seventy. You are to have special care that the old fox and his sons doe upon no account escape your hands. You are to secure all the avenues, that no man escape. This you are to put in execution att five o'clock in the morning precisely, and by that time, or very shortly after it, I'll strive to be att you with a stronger party. If I doe not come to you at five, you are not to tarry for me, but to fall on. This is by the king's speciall command,

for the good and safety of the country, that these mis-
creants be cutt off root and branch. See that this be putt
in execution without feud or favour, else you may expect
to be treated as not true to the king's government, nor a
man fitt to carry a commission in the king's service.
Expecting you will not faill in the fulfilling hereof as you
love yourself, I subscribe these with my hand.
                                    "ROBERT DUNCANSON.

" *For their Majesty's service.*
" *To Captain Robert Campbell of Glenlyon.*"

This order was but too literally obeyed. At the
appointed hour, when the whole inhabitants of
the glen were asleep, the work of murder began.
M'Ian was one of the first who fell. Drummond's
narrative fills up the remainder of the dreadful
story.

"They then served all within the family in the
same manner, without distinction of age or person.
In a word—for the horror of that execrable butchery
must give pain to the reader—they left none alive
but a young child, who, being frighted with the
noise of the guns, and the dismal shrieks and cries
of its dying parents, whom they were a-murdering,
got hold of Captain Campbell's knees, and wrapt
itself within his cloak ; by which, chancing to move
compassion, the captain inclined to have saved it,
but one Drummond, an officer, arriving about the
break of day with more troops, commanded it to
be shot by a file of musqueteers. Nothing could
be more shocking and horrible than the prospect
of these houses bestrewed with mangled bodies of
the dead, covered with blood, and resounding with
the groans of wretches in the last agonies of life.

"Two sons of Glencoe's were the only persons
that escaped in that quarter of the country ; for,
growing jealous of some ill designs from the be-
haviour of the soldiers, they stole from their beds
a few minutes before the tragedy began, and,
chancing to overhear two of them discoursing
plainly of the matter, they endeavoured to have
advertised their father, but, finding that imprac-

ticable, they ran to the other end of the country and alarmed the inhabitants. There was another accident that contributed much to their safety; for the night was so excessively stormy and tempestuous, that four hundred soldiers, who were appointed to murder these people, were stopped in their march from Inverlochy, and could not get up till they had time to save themselves. To cover the deformity of so dreadful a sight, the soldiers burned all the houses to the ground, after having rifled them, carried away nine hundred cows, two hundred horses, numberless herds of sheep and goats, and everything else that belonged to these miserable people. Lamentable was the case of the women and children that escaped the butchery: the mountains were covered with a deep snow, the rivers impassable, storm and tempest filled the air, and added to the horrors and darkness of the night, and there were no houses to shelter them within many miles." *

Such was the awful massacre of Glencoe, an event which has left an indelible and execrable stain upon the memory of William of Orange. The records of Indian warfare can hardly afford a parallel instance of atrocity; and this deed, coupled with his deliberate treachery in the Darien scheme, whereby Scotland was for a time absolutely ruined, is sufficient to account for the little estimation in which the name of the "great Whig deliverer" is still regarded in the valleys of the North.

Memoirs of Sir Ewen Cameron of Locheill.

THE WIDOW OF GLENCOE.

Do not lift him from the bracken,
    Leave him lying where he fell—
Better bier ye cannot fashion :
    None beseems him half so well
As the bare and broken heather,
    And the hard and trampled sod,
Whence his angry soul ascended
    To the judgment-seat of God !
Winding-sheet we cannot give him—
    Seek no mantle for the dead,
Save the cold and spotless covering
    Showered from heaven upon his head.
Leave his broadsword, as we found it,
    Bent and broken with the blow,
That, before he died, avenged him
    On the foremost of the foe.
Leave the blood upon his bosom—
    Wash not off that sacred stain ;
Let it stiffen on the tartan,
    Let his wounds unclosed remain,
Till the day when he shall show them
    At the throne of God on high,
When the murderer and the murdered
    Meet before their Judge's eye !

Nay—ye should not weep, my children !
    Leave it to the faint and weak ;
Sobs are but a woman's weapon—
    Tears befit a maiden's cheek.
Weep not, children of Macdonald !
    Weep not thou, his orphan heir—

Not in shame, but stainless honour,
  Lies thy slaughtered father there.
Weep not—but when years are over,
  And thine arm is strong and sure
And thy foot is swift and steady
  On the mountain and the muir—
Let thy heart be hard as iron,
  And thy wrath as fierce as fire,
Till the hour when vengeance cometh
  For the race that slew thy sire !
Till in deep and dark Glenlyon
  Rise a louder shriek of woe,
Than at midnight, from their eyrie,
  Scared the eagles of Glencoe :
Louder than the screams that mingled
  With the howling of the blast,
When the murderer's steel was clashing,
  And the fires were rising fast ;
When thy noble father bounded
  To the rescue of his men,
And the slogan of our kindred
  Pealed throughout the startled glen ;
When the herd of frantic women
  Stumbled through the midnight snow,
With their fathers' houses blazing,
  And their dearest dead below !
Oh, the horror of the tempest,
  As the flashing drift was blown,
Crimsoned with the conflagration,
  And the roofs went thundering down !
Oh, the prayers—the prayers and curses
  That together winged their flight
From the maddened hearts of many
  Through that long and woeful night !
Till the fires began to dwindle,
  And the shots grew faint and few,
And we heard the foemen's challenge
  Only in a far balloo :
Till the silence once more settled
  O'er the gorges of the glen,
Broken only by the Cona

Plunging through its naked den.
Slowly from the mountain-summit
  Was the drifting veil withdrawn,
And the ghastly valley glimmered
  In the gray December dawn.
Better had the morning never
  Dawned upon our dark despair !
Black amidst the common whiteness
  Rose the spectral ruins there :
But the sight of these was nothing
  More than wrings the wild-dove's breast,
When she searches for her offspring
  Round the relics of her nest.
For in many a spot the tartan
  Peered above the wintry heap,
Marking where a dead Macdonald
  Lay within his frozen sleep.
Tremblingly we scooped the covering
  From each kindred victim's head,
And the living lips were burning
  On the cold ones of the dead.
And I left them with their dearest—
  Dearest charge had every one—
Left the maiden with her lover,
  Left the mother with her son.
I alone of all was mateless—
  Far more wretched I than they,
For the snow would not discover
  Where my lord and husband lay.
But I wandered up the valley,
  Till I found him lying low,
With the gash upon his bosom
  And the frown upon his brow—
Till I found him lying murdered,
  Where he wooed me long ago !
Woman's weakness shall not shame me
  Why should I have tears to shed ?
Could I rain them down like water,
  O my hero ! on thy head—
Could the cry of lamentation
  Wake thee from thy silent sleep,

Could it set thy heart a throbbing,
 It were mine to wail and weep!
But I will not waste my sorrow,
 Lest the Campbell women say
That the daughters of Clanranald
 Are as weak and frail as they.
I had wept thee, hadst thou fallen,
 Like our fathers, on thy shield,
When a host of English foemen
 Camped upon a Scottish field—
I had mourned thee, hadst thou perished
 With the foremost of his name,
When the valiant and the noble
 Died around the dauntless Græme!
But I will not wrong thee, husband!
 With my unavailing cries,
Whilst thy cold and mangled body,
 Stricken by the traitor, lies;
Whilst he counts the gold and glory
 That this hideous night has won,
And his heart is big with triumph
 At the murder he has done.
Other eyes than mine shall glisten,
 Other hearts be rent in twain,
Ere the heathbells on thy hillock
 Wither in the autumn rain.
Then I'll seek thee where thou sleepest,
 And I'll veil my weary head,
Praying for a place beside thee,
 Dearer than my bridal-bed:
And I'll give thee tears, my husband!
 If the tears remain to me,
When the widows of the foemen
 Cry the coronach for thee!

✤

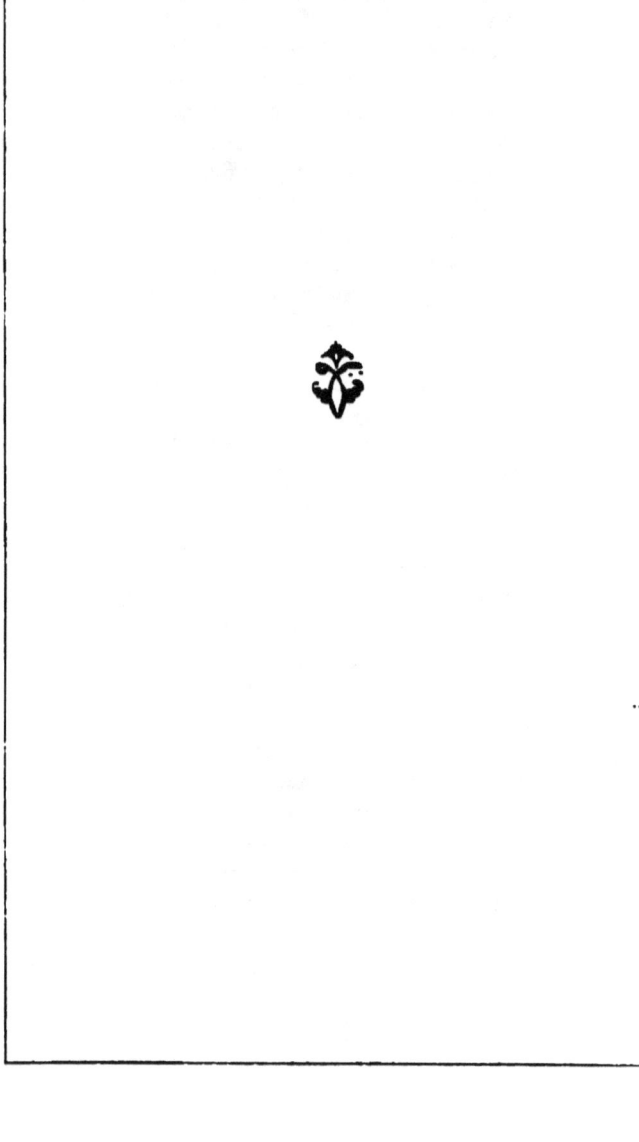

The Island of the Scots.

In consequence of a capitulation with Government, the regular troops who had served under Lord Dundee were transhipped to France ; and, immediately upon their landing, the officers and others had their rank confirmed according to the tenor of the commissions and characters which they bore in Scotland. They were distributed throughout the different garrisons in the north of France, and, though nominally in the service of King James, derived their whole means of subsistence from the bounty of the French monarch. So long as it appeared probable that another descent was meditated, those gentlemen, who were almost without exception men of considerable family, assented to this arrangement ; but the destruction of the French fleet under Admiral Tourville, off La Hogue, led to a material change in their views. After that naval engagement, it became obvious that the cause of the fugitive King was in the meantime desperate, and the Scottish officers, with no less gallantry than honour, volunteered a sacrifice which, so far as I know, has hardly been equalled.

The old and interesting pamphlet written by one of the corps,* from which I have extracted most of the following details, but which is seldom perused except by the antiquary, states that—" The Scottish officers considering that, by the loss of the French fleet, King James's restoration would be retarded

* An Account of Dundee's Officers, after they went to France. By an Officer of the Army. London, 1714.

for some time, and that they were burdensome to the King of France, being entertained in garrisons on whole pay, without doing duty, when he had almost all Europe in confederacy against him; therefore humbly entreated King James to have them reduced into a company of private sentinels, and choose officers amongst themselves to command them; assuring his majesty that they would serve in the meanest circumstances, and undergo the greatest hardships and fatigues, that reason could imagine or misfortunes inflict, until it pleased God to restore him. King James commended their generosity and loyalty, but disapproved of what they proposed, and told them it was impossible that gentlemen, who had served in so honourable posts as formerly they had enjoyed, and lived in so great plenty and ease, could ever undergo the fatigue and hardships of private sentinels' duty. Again, that his own first command was a company of officers, whereof several died; others, wearied with fatigue, drew their discharges; till at last it dwindled into nothing, and he got no reputation by the command: therefore he desired them to insist no more on that project. The officers (notwithstanding his majesty's desire to the contrary) made several interests at court, and harassed him so much, that at last he condescended," and appointed those who were to command them.

Shortly afterwards, the new corps was reviewed for the first and last time by the unfortunate James in the gardens of Saint Germains, and the tears are said to have gushed from his eyes at the sight of so many brave men, reduced, through their disinterested and persevering loyalty, to so very humble a condition. "Gentlemen," said he, "my own misfortunes are not so nigh my heart as yours. It grieves me beyond what I can express, to see so many brave and worthy gentlemen, who had once the prospect of being the chief officers in my army, reduced to the stations of private sentinels. Nothing but your loyalty, and that of a few of my subjects in Britain, who are forced from their allegiance by the Prince of Orange, and who, I know, will be ready on all occasions to serve me and my distressed family, could make me willing to live. The sense of what all of you have done and undergone for your loyalty, hath made so deep an impression upon my heart, that if it ever please God to restore me, it is impossible I can be forgetful of your services and sufferings. Neither can there be any posts in the armies of my dominions but what you have just pretensions to. As for my son, your Prince, he is of your own blood, a child capable of any impression, and, as his education will be from you, it is not supposable that he can forget your merits. At your own desires you are now going a long march far distant from me. Fear God and love one another. Write your wants particularly to me, and depend upon it always to find me your parent and King." The scene bore a strong resemblance to one which many years afterwards occurred at Fontainebleau. The company listened to his words with deep emotion, gathered round him, as if half repentant of their own desire to go; and so parted, for ever on this earth, the dethroned monarch and his exiled subjects.

The number of this company of officers was about one hundred and twenty: their destination was Perpignan in Rousillon, close upon the frontier of Spain, where they were to join the army under the command of the Mareschal de Noailles. Their power of endurance, though often most severely tested in an unwholesome climate, seems to have been no less remarkable than their gallantry, which upon many occasions called forth the warm acknowledgment of the French commanders. "*Le gentilhomme,*" said one of the generals, in acknowledgment of their readiness at a peculiarly critical moment, "*est toujours gentilhomme, et se montre toujours tel dans besoin et dans le danger*" —a eulogy as applicable to them as it was in later days to La Tour d'Auvergne, styled the first grenadier of France. At Perpignan they were joined by two other Scottish companies, and the three seem to have continued to serve together for several campaigns.

As a proof of the estimation in which they were held, I shall merely extract a short account of the taking of Rosas in Catalonia, before referring to the exploit which forms the subject of the following ballad. " On the 27th of May, the company of officers, and other Scottish companies, were joined by two companies of Irish, to make up a battalion in order to mount the trenches; and the major part of the officers listed themselves in the company of grenadiers, under the command of the brave Major Rutherford, who, on his way to the trenches, in sight of Mareschal de Noailles and his court, marched with his company on the side of the trench, which exposed him to the fire of a bastion, where there were two culverins and several other guns planted; likewise to the fire of two curtins lined with small shot. Colonel Brown, following with the battalion, was obliged, in honour, to march the same way Major Rutherford had done; the danger whereof the Mareschal immediately perceiving, ordered one of his aides-de-camp to command Rutherford to march under cover of the trench, which he did; and if he had but delayed six minutes, the grenadiers and battalion had been cut to pieces. Rutherford, with his grenadiers, marched to a trench near the town, and the battalion to a trench on the rear and flank of the grenadiers, who fired so incessantly on the besieged, that they thought (the trench being practicable) they were going to make their attacks, immediately beat a chamade, and were willing to give up the town upon reasonable terms: but the Mareschal's demands were so exorbitant, that the Governor could not agree to them. Then firing began on both sides to be very hot; and they in the town, seeing how the grenadiers lay, killed eight of them. When the Governor surrendered the town, he inquired of the Mareschal what countrymen these grenadiers were; and assured him it was on their account he delivered up the town, because they fired so hotly, that he believed they were resolved to attack the breach. He answered, smiling, 'Ces sont mes enfans—They are my children.' Again; 'they are the King of Great Britain's Scottish officers, who, to show their willingness to share of his miseries, have reduced themselves to the carrying of arms, and chosen to serve under my command.' The next day, when the Mareschal rode along the front of the camp, he halted at the company of the officers' piquet, and they all surrounded him. Then, with his hat in his hand, he thanked them for their good services in the trenches, and freely acknowledged it was their conduct and courage which compelled the Governor to give up the town; and assured them he would acquaint his master with the same, which he did. For when his son arrived with the news at Versailles, the King, having read the letter, immediately took coach to St. Germains; and when he had shown King James the letter, he thanked him for the services his subjects had done in taking Rosas in Catalonia; who, with concern, replied, they were the stock of his British officers, and that he was sorry he could not make better provision for them."

And a miserable provision it was! They were gradually compelled to part with every remnant of the property which they had secured from the ruins of their fortunes; so that when they arrived, after various adventures, at Scelestat, in Alsace, they were literally without the common means of subsistence. Famine and the sword had, by this time, thinned their ranks, but had not diminished their spirit, as the following narrative of their last exploit will show:—

"In December 1697, General Stirk, who com-

manded for the Germans, appeared with 16,000
men on the other side of the Rhine, which obliged
the Marquis de Sell to draw out all the garrisons in
Alsace, who made up about 4000 men ; and he
encamped on the other side of the Rhine, over
against General Stirk, to prevent his passing the
Rhine, and carrying a bridge over into an island
in the middle of it, which the French foresaw would
be of great prejudice to them. For the enemy's
guns, placed on that island, would extremely gall
their camp, which they could not hinder for the
deepness of the water and their wanting of boats—
for which the Marquis quickly sent ; but arriving
too late, the Germans had carried a bridge over
into the island, where they had posted above five
hundred men, who, by order of their engineers,
entrenched themselves : which the company of
officers perceiving, who always grasped after
honour, and scorned all thoughts of danger, resolved to wade the river, and attack the Germans
in the island ; and for that effect, desired Captain
John Foster, who then commanded them, to beg of
the Marquis that they might have liberty to attack
the Germans in the island ; who told Captain
Foster, when the boats came up, they should be
the first that attacked. Foster courteously thanked
the Marquis, and told him they would wade into
the island, who shrunk up his shoulders, prayed
God to bless them, and desired them to do what
they pleased." Whereupon the officers, with the
other two Scottish companies, made themselves
ready ; and having secured their arms round their
necks, waded into the river hand-in-hand, "according to the Highland fashion," with the water as high
as their breasts ; and having crossed the heavy
stream, fell upon the Germans in their entrench-
ment. These were presently thrown into confusion,
and retreated, breaking down their own bridges,
whilst many of them were drowned. This movement, having been made in the dusk of the evening, partook of the character of a surprise ; but it

appears to me a very remarkable one, as having been effected under such circumstances, in the dead of winter, and in the face of an enemy who possessed the advantages both of position and of numerical superiority. The author of the narrative adds:— "When the Marquis de Sell heard the firing, and understood that the Germans were beat out of the island, he made the sign of the cross on his face and breast, and declared publicly, that it was the bravest action that ever he saw, and that his army had no honour by it. As soon as the boats came, the Marquis sent into the island to acquaint the officers that he would send them both troops and provisions, who thanked his Excellency, and desired he should be informed that they wanted no troops, and could not spare time to make use of provisions, and only desired spades, shovels, and pickaxes, wherewith they might intrench themselves—which were immediately sent to them. The next morning, the Marquis came into the island, and kindly embraced every officer, and thanked them for the good service they had done his master, assuring them he would write a true account of their honour and bravery to the Court of France, which, at the reading his letters, immediately went to St. Germains, and thanked King James for the services his subjects had done on the Rhine."

The company kept possession of the island for nearly six weeks, notwithstanding repeated attempts on the part of the Germans to surprise and dislodge them; but all these having been defeated by the extreme watchfulness of the Scots, General Stirk at length drew off his army and retreated. "In consequence of this action," says the chronicler, "that island is called at present Isle d'Ecosse, and will in likelihood bear that name until the general conflagration."

Two years afterwards, a treaty of peace was concluded; and this gallant company of soldiers, worthy of a better fate, was broken up and dispersed. At the time when the narrative, from

F.

which I have quoted so freely, was compiled, not more than sixteen of Dundee's veterans were alive. The author concludes thus,—"And thus was dissolved one of the best companies that ever marched under command! Gentlemen, who, in the midst of all their pressures and obscurity, never forgot they were gentlemen; and whom the sweets of a brave, a just, and honourable conscience, rendered perhaps more happy under those sufferings, than the most prosperous and triumphant in iniquity, since our minds stamp our happiness."

Some years ago, while visiting the ancient Scottish convent at Ratisbon, my attention was drawn to the monumental inscriptions on the walls of the dormitory, many of which bear reference to gentlemen of family and distinction, whose political principles had involved them in the troubles of 1688, 1715, and 1745. Whether the cloister which now holds their dust had afforded them a shelter in the later years of their misfortunes, I know not; but for one that is so commemorated, hundreds of the exiles must have passed away in obscurity, buried in the field on which they fell, or carried from the damp vaults of the military hospital to the trench, without any token of remembrance, or any other wish beyond that which the minstrels have ascribed to one of the greatest of our olden heroes—

> "Oh bury me by the bracken bush,
> Beneath the blooming brier:
> Let never living mortal ken
> That a kindly Scot lies here!"

THE ISLAND OF THE SCOTS.

I.

THE Rhine is running deep and red,
　　The island lies before—
"Now is there one of all the host
　　Will dare to venture o'er?
For not alone the river's sweep
　　Might make a brave man quail:
The foe are on the further side,
　　Their shot comes fast as hail.
God help us, if the middle isle
　　We may not hope to win!
Now, is there any of the host
　　Will dare to venture in?"

II.

"The ford is deep, the banks are steep,
　　The island-shore lies wide:
Nor man nor horse could stem its force
　　Or reach the further side.
See there! amidst the willow boughs
　　The serried bayonets gleam;
They've flung their bridge—they've won the isle;
　　The foe have crossed the stream!
Their volley flashes sharp and strong—
　　By all the Saints, I trow,
There never yet was soldier born
　　Could force that passage now!"

III.

So spoke the bold French Mareschal
　　With him who led the van,
Whilst rough and red before their view
　　The turbid river ran.

Nor bridge nor boat had they to cross
   The wild and swollen Rhine,
And thundering on the other bank
   Far stretched the German line.
Hard by there stood a swarthy man
   Was leaning on his sword,
And a saddened smile lit up his face
   As he heard the Captain's word.
" I've seen a wilder stream ere now
   Than that which rushes there ;
I've stemmed a heavier torrent yet
   And never thought to dare.
If German steel be sharp and keen,
   Is ours not strong and true ?
There may be danger in the deed,
   But there is honour too."

IV.

The old lord in his saddle turned,
   And hastily he said—
" Hath bold Duguesclin's fiery heart
   Awakened from the dead ?
Thou art the leader of the Scots—
   Now well and sure I know,
That gentle blood in dangerous hour
   Ne'er yet ran cold nor slow,
And I have seen ye in the fight
   Do all that mortal may :
If honour is the boon ye seek
   It may be won this day.
The prize is in the middle isle,
   There lies the venturous way ;
And armies twain are on the plain,
   The daring deed to see—
Now ask thy gallant company
   If they will follow thee !"

V.

Right gladsome looked the Captain then,
   And nothing did he say,

But he turned him to his little band—
  Oh few, I ween, were they!
The relics of the bravest force
  That ever fought in fray.
No one of all that company
  But bore a gentle name,
Not one whose fathers had not stood
  In Scotland's fields of fame.
All they had marched with great Dundee
  To where he fought and fell,
And in the deadly battle-strife
  Had venged their leader well;
And they had bent the knee to earth
  When every eye was dim,
As o'er their hero's buried corpse
  They sang the funeral hymn;
And they had trod the Pass once more,
  And stooped on either side
To pluck the heather from the spot
  Where he had dropped and died;
And they had bound it next their hearts,
  And ta'en a last farewell
Of Scottish earth and Scottish sky,
  Where Scotland's glory fell.
Then went they forth to foreign lands
  Like bent and broken men,
Who leave their dearest hope behind,
  And may not turn again!

VI.

"The stream," he said, "is broad and deep,
  And stubborn is the foe—
Yon island-strength is guarded well—
  Say, brothers, will ye go?
From home and kin for many a year
  Our steps have wandered wide,
And never may our bones be laid
  Our fathers' graves beside.
No sisters have we to lament,
  No wives to wail our fall;

The traitor's and the spoiler's hand
   Have reft our hearths of all.
But we have hearts, and we have arms
   As strong to will and dare
As when our ancient banners flew
   Within the northern air.
Come, brothers! let me name a spell
   Shall rouse your souls again,
And send the old blood bounding free
   Through pulse, and heart, and vein!
Call back the days of bygone years—
   Be young and strong once more;
Think yonder stream, so stark and red,
   Is one we've crossed before.
Rise, hill and glen! rise, crag and wood!
   Rise up on either hand—
Again upon the Garry's banks,
   On Scottish soil we stand!
Again I see the tartans wave,
   Again the trumpets ring;
Again I hear our leader's call—
   'Upon them, for the King!'
Stayed we behind that glorious day
   For roaring flood or linn?
The soul of Græme is with us still—
   Now, brothers! will ye in?

VII.

No stay—no pause.   With one accord
   They grasped each other's hand,
And plunged into the angry flood,
   That bold and dauntless band.
High flew the spray above their heads
   Yet onward still they bore,
Midst cheer, and shout, and answering yell,
   And shot and cannon roar.
"Now by the Holy Cross! I swear,
   Since earth and sea began
Was never such a daring deed
   Essayed by mortal man!"

VIII.

Thick blew the smoke across the stream,
  And faster flashed the flame :
The water plashed in hissing jets
  As ball and bullet came.
Yet onwards pushed the Cavaliers
  All stern and undismayed,
With thousand armèd foes before,
  And none behind to aid.
Once, as they neared the middle stream,
  So strong the torrent swept,
That scarce that long and living wall,
  Their dangerous footing kept.
Then rose a warning cry behind,
  A joyous shout before :
" The current's strong—the way is long—
  They'll never reach the shore !
See, see ! They stagger in the midst,
  They waver in their line !
Fire on the madmen ! break their ranks,
  And whelm them in the Rhine !"

IX.

Have you seen the tall trees swaying
  When the blast is piping shrill,
And the whirlwind reels in fury
  Down the gorges of the hill?
How they toss their mighty branches,
  Striving with the tempest's shock ;
How they keep their place of vantage,
  Cleaving firmly to the rock?
Even so the Scottish warriors
  Held their own against the river ;
Though the water flashed around them,
  Not an eye was seen to quiver ;
Though the shot flew sharp and deadly,
  Not a man relaxed his hold :
For their hearts were big and thrilling
  With the mighty thoughts of old.

One word was spoke among them,
    And through the ranks it spread—
" Remember our dead Claverhouse ! "
    Was all the Captain said.
Then, sternly bending forward,
    They struggled on awhile,
Until they cleared the heavy stream,
    Then rushed towards the isle.

X.

The German heart is stout and true,
    The German arm is strong ;
The German foot goes seldom back
    Where armèd foemen throng.
But never had they faced in field
    So stern a charge before,
And never had they felt the sweep
    Of Scotland's broad claymore.
Not fiercer pours the avalanche
    Adown the steep incline,
That rises o'er the parent-springs
    Of rough and rapid Rhine—
Scarce swifter shoots the bolt from heaven
    Than came the Scottish band,
Right up against the guarded trench,
    And o'er it, sword in hand.
In vain their leaders forward press—
    They meet the deadly brand !
O lonely island of the Rhine,
    Where seed was never sown,
What harvest lay upon thy sands,
    By those strong reapers thrown ?
What saw the winter moon that night,
    As, struggling through the rain,
She poured a wan and fitful light
    On marsh, and stream, and plain ?
A dreary spot with corpses strewn,
    And bayonets glistening round ;
A broken bridge, a stranded boat,
    A bare and battered mound ;

And one huge watch-fire's kindled pile,
  That sent its quivering glare
To tell the leaders of the host
  The conquering Scots were there!

XI.

And did they twine the laurel-wreath
  For those who fought so well?
And did they honour those who lived,
  And weep for those who fell?
What meed of thanks was given to them
  Let aged annals tell.
Why should they twine the laurel-wreath—
  Why crown the cup with wine?
It was not Frenchmen's blood that flowed
  So freely on the Rhine—
A stranger band of beggared men
  Had done the venturous deed:
The glory was to France alone,
  The danger was their meed.
And what cared they for idle thanks
  From foreign prince and peer?
What virtue had such honied words
  The exiles' hearts to cheer?
What mattered it that men should vaunt
  And loud and fondly swear,
That higher feat of chivalry
  Was never wrought elsewhere?
They bore within their breasts the grief
  That fame can never heal—
The deep, unutterable woe
  Which none save exiles feel.
Their hearts were yearning for the land
  They ne'er might see again—
For Scotland's high and heathered hills,
  For mountain, loch, and glen—
For those who haply lay at rest
  Beyond the distant sea,
Beneath the green and daisied turf
  Where they would gladly be!

E 2

XII.

Long years went by.   The lonely isle
  In Rhine's impetuous flood
Has ta'en another name from those
  Who bought it with their blood :
And though the legend does not live,
  For legends lightly die,
The peasant, as he sees the stream
  In winter rolling by,
And foaming o'er its channel-bed
  Between him and the spot
Won by the warriors of the sword,
Still calls that deep and dangerous ford
  The Passage of the Scot.

CHARLES EDWARD AT VERSAILLES.

THOUGH the sceptre had departed from the House of Stuart, it was reserved for one of its last descendants to prove to the world, by his personal gallantry and noble spirit of enterprise, that he at least had not degenerated from his royal line of ancestors. The daring effort of Charles Edward to recover the crown of these kingdoms for his father, is to us the most remarkable incident of the last century. It was honourable alike to the Prince and to those who espoused his cause; and, even in a political point of view, the outbreak ought not to be deplored, since its failure put an end for ever to the dynastical struggle which, for more than half a century, had agitated the whole of Britain, established the rule of law and of social order throughout the mountainous districts of Scotland, and blended Celt and Saxon into one prosperous and united people. It was better that the antiquated system of clanship should have expired in a blaze of glory, than gradually dwindled into contempt; better that the patriarchal rule should at once have been extinguished by the dire catastrophe of Culloden, than that it should have lingered on, the shadow of an old tradition. There is nothing now to prevent us from dwelling with pride and admiration on the matchless devotion displayed by the Highlanders, in 1745, in behalf of the heir of him whom they acknowledged as their lawful king. No feeling can arise to repress the interest and the sympathy which is excited by the perusal of the tale narrating the sufferings of the princely wanderer. That unbought loyalty and allegiance of the heart, which would not depart from its constancy until the tomb of the Vatican had closed upon the last of the Stuart line, has long since been transferred to the constitutional sovereign of these realms; and the enthusiastic welcome which has so often greeted the return of Queen Victoria to her Highland home, owes its origin to a deeper feeling than that dull respect which modern liberalism asserts to be the only tribute due to the first magistrate of the land.

The campaign of 1745 yields in romantic interest to none which is written in history. A young and inexperienced prince, whose person was utterly unknown to any of his adherents, landed on the west coast of Scotland, not at the head of a foreign force, not munimented with supplies and arms, but accompanied by a mere handful of followers, and ignorant of the language of the people amongst whom he was hazarding his person. His presence in Scotland had not been urged by the chiefs of the clans, most of whom were deeply averse to embarking in an enterprise which must involve them in a war with so powerful an antagonist as England, and which, if unsuccessful, could only terminate in the utter ruin of their fortunes. This was not a cause in which the whole of Scotland was concerned. Although it was well known that many leading families in the Lowlands entertained Jacobite opinions, and although a large proportion of the common people had not yet become reconciled to, or satisfied of the advantages of the Union, by which they considered themselves dishonoured and betrayed, it was hardly to be expected that, without some fair guarantee for success, the bulk of the Scottish nation would actively bestir themselves on the side of the exiled family. Besides this, even amongst the Highlanders there was not unanimity of opinion. The three northern

clans of Sutherland, Mackay, and Monro, were
known to be staunch supporters of the Government. It was doubtful what part might be taken
in the struggle by those of Mackenzie and Ross.
The chiefs of Skye, who could have brought
a large force of armed men into the field, had
declined participating in the attempt. The assistance of Lord Lovat, upon whom the co-operation
of the Frasers might depend, could not be calculated on with certainty; and nothing but hos-
tility could be expected from the powerful sept
of the Campbells. Under such circumstances, it
is little wonder if Cameron of Locheill, the most
sagacious of all the chieftains who favoured the
Stuart cause, was struck with consternation and
alarm at the news of the Prince's landing, or
that he attempted to persuade him from undertaking an adventure so seemingly hopeless. Mr.
Robert Chambers, in his admirable history of that
period, does not in the least exaggerate the importance of the interview, on the result of which
the prosecution of the war depended. "On arriving at Borrodale, Locheill had a private interview with the Prince, in which the probabilities
of the enterprise were anxiously debated. Charles
used every argument to excite the loyalty of
Locheill, and the chief exerted all his eloquence
to persuade the Prince to withdraw till a better
opportunity. Charles represented the present as
the best possible opportunity, seeing that the
French general kept the British army completely
engaged abroad, while at home there were no
troops but one or two newly-raised regiments.
He expressed his confidence that a small body of
Highlanders would be sufficient to gain a victory
over all the force that could now be brought
against him; and he was equally sure that such
an advantage was all that was required to make
his friends at home declare in his favour, and
cause those abroad to send him assistance. All
he wanted was that the Highlanders should begin

the war. Locheill still resisted, entreating Charles
to be more temperate, and consent to remain concealed where he was, till his friends should meet
together and concert what was best to be done.
Charles, whose mind was wound up to the utmost
pitch of impatience, paid no regard to this proposal,
but answered that he was determined to put all to
the hazard. 'In a few days,' said he, 'with the
few friends I have, I will raise the royal standard,
and proclaim to the people of Britain that Charles
Stuart is come over to claim the crown of his
ancestors—to win it, or to perish in the attempt !
Locheill—who, my father has often told me, was
our firmest friend—may stay at home, and learn
from the newspapers the fate of his Prince !'
'No!' said Locheill, stung by so poignant a
reproach, and hurried away by the enthusiasm
of the moment; 'I will share the fate of my
Prince, and so shall every man over whom nature
or fortune has given me any power.' Such was
the juncture upon which depended the civil war
of 1745; for it is a point agreed, says Mr. Home,
who narrates this conversation, that if Locheill
had persisted in his refusal to take arms, no
other chief would have joined the standard, and
the spark of rebellion must have been instantly
extinguished." Not more than twelve hundred
men were assembled in Glenfinnan on the day
when the standard was unfurled by the Marquis
of Tullibardine ; and, at the head of this mere
handful of followers, Charles Edward commenced
the stupendous enterprise of reconquering the
dominions of his fathers.

With a force which, at the battle of Preston, did
not double the above numbers, the Prince descended upon the Lowlands, having baffled the
attempts of General Cope to intercept his march—
occupied the city of Perth and the town of Dundee,
and finally, after a faint show of resistance on the
part of the burghers, took possession of the ancient
capital of Scotland, and once more established a

court in the halls of Holyrood. His youth, his
gallantry, and the grace and beauty of his person,
added to a most winning and affable address,
acquired for him the sympathy of many who, from
political motives, abstained from becoming his adherents. Possibly certain feelings of nationality,
which no deliberate views of civil or religious policy
could altogether extirpate, led such men to regard,
with a sensation akin to pride, the spectacle of a
prince descended from the long line of Scottish
kings, again occupying his ancestral seat, and
restoring to their country, which had been utterly
neglected by the new dynasty, a portion of its
former state. No doubt a sense of pity for the
probable fate of one so young and chivalrous was
often present to their minds, for they had thorough
confidence in the intrepidity of the regular troops,
and in the capacity of their commander ; and they
never for a moment supposed that these could be
successfully encountered by a raw levy of undisci-
plined Highlanders, ill-armed and worse equipped,
and without the support of any artillery.

The issue of the battle of Prestonpans struck
Edinburgh with amazement. In point of numbers
the two armies were nearly equal, but in everything
else, save personal valour, the royal troops had the
advantage. And yet, *in four minutes*—for the
battle is said not to have lasted longer—the Highlanders having only made one terrific and impetuous charge—the rout of the regulars was general.
The infantry was broken and cut to pieces ; the
dragoons, who behaved shamefully on the occasion,
turned bridle and fled, without having once crossed
swords with the enemy. Mr. Chambers thus termi-
nates his account of the action : "The general
result of the battle of Preston may be stated as
having been the total overthrow and almost entire
destruction of the royal army. Most of the infantry,
falling upon the park walls of Preston, were there
huddled together, without the power of resistance,
into a confused drove, and had either to surrender

or to be cut to pieces.   Many, in vainly attempting
to climb over the walls, fell an easy prey to the
ruthless claymore.   Nearly 400, it is said, were
thus slain, 700 taken, while only about 170 in all
succeeded in effecting their escape.

" The dragoons, with worse conduct, were much
more fortunate.   In falling back, they had the
good luck to find outlets from their respective
positions by the roads which ran along the various
extremities of the park wall, and they thus got
clear through the village with little slaughter ;
after which, as the Highlanders had no horse to
pursue them, they were safe.   Several officers,
among whom were Fowkes and Lascelles, escaped
to Cockenzie and along Seton Sands, in a direction
contrary to the general flight.

" The unfortunate Cope had attempted, at the
first break of Gardiner's dragoons, to stop and
rally them, but was borne headlong, with the
confused bands, through the narrow road to the
south of the enclosures, notwithstanding all his
efforts to the contrary.   On getting beyond the
village, where he was joined by the retreating
bands of the other regiment, he made one anxious
effort, with the Earls of Loudoun and Home, to
form and bring them back to charge the enemy,
now disordered by the pursuit ; but in vain.
They fled on, ducking their heads along their
horses' necks to escape the bullets which the
pursuers occasionally sent after them.   By using
great exertions, and holding pistols to the heads
of the troopers, Sir John and a few of his officers
induced a small number of them to halt in a field
near St. Clement's Wells, about two miles from
the battle-ground.   But, after a momentary delay,
the accidental firing of a pistol renewed the panic,
and they rode off once more in great disorder.
Sir John Cope, with a portion of them, reached
Channelkirk at an early hour in the forenoon, and
there halted to breakfast, and to write a brief note
to one of the state-officers, relating the fate of the

day. He then resumed his flight, and reached
Coldstream that night. Next morning he proceeded to Berwick, whose fortifications seemed
competent to give the security he required. He
everywhere brought the first tidings of his own
defeat."

This victory operated very much in favour of
Prince Charles. It secured him, for a season, the
undisputed possession of Scotland, and enabled
numerous adherents from all parts of the country
to raise such forces as they could command, and
to repair to his banner. His popularity in Edinburgh daily increased, as the qualities of his
person and mind became known; and such testimony as the following, with respect to his estimation by the fair sex, and the devotion they exhibited
in his cause, is not overcharged. "His affability
and great personal grace wrought him high favour
with the ladies, who, as we learn from the letters
of President Forbes, became generally so zealous
in his cause, as to have some serious effect in
inducing their admirers to declare for the Prince.
There was, we know for certain, a Miss Lumsden,
who plainly told her lover, a young artist, named
Robert Strange, that he might think no more
of her unless he should immediately join Prince
Charles, and thus actually prevailed upon him
to take up arms. It may be added that he survived the enterprise, escaped with great difficulty,
and married the lady. He was afterwards the
best line-engraver of his time, and received the
honour of knighthood from George III. White
ribbons and breastknots became at this time conspicuous articles of female attire in private assemblies. The ladies also showed considerable
zeal in contributing plate and other articles for
the use of the Chevalier at the palace, and in
raising pecuniary subsidies for him. Many a
posset-dish and snuff-box, many a treasured neck-
lace and repeater, many a jewel which had adorned
its successive generations of family beauties, was

at this time sold or laid in pledge, to raise a little money for the service of Prince Charlie."

As to the motives and intended policy of this remarkable and unfortunate young man, it may be interesting to quote the terms of the proclamation which he issued on the 10th October 1745, before commencing his march into England. Let his history be impartially read, his character, as spoken to by those who knew him best, fairly noted, and I think there cannot be a doubt that, had he succeeded in his daring attempt, he would have been true to the letter of his word, and fulfilled a pledge which Britain never more required than at the period when that document was penned :—

"Do not the pulpits and congregations of the clergy, as well as your weekly papers, ring with the dreadful threats of popery, slavery, tyranny, and arbitrary power, which are now ready to be imposed upon you by the formidable powers of France and Spain? Is not my royal father represented as a bloodthirsty tyrant, breathing out nothing but destruction to all who will not immediately embrace an odious religion? Or have I myself been better used? But listen only to the naked truth.

"I, with my own money, hired a small vessel. Ill-supplied with money, arms, or friends, I arrived in Scotland, attended by seven persons. I publish the King my father's declaration, and proclaim his title, with pardon in one hand, and in the other liberty of conscience, and the most solemn promises to grant whatever a free Parliament shall propose for the happiness of a people. I have, I confess, the greatest reason to adore the goodness of Almighty God, who has in so remarkable a manner protected me and my small army through the many dangers to which we were at first exposed, and who has led me in the way to victory, and to the capital of this ancient kingdom, amidst the acclamations of the King my father's subjects. Why, then, is so much pains taken to spirit up the minds of the people against this my undertaking?

"The reason is obvious; it is, lest the real sense of the nation's present sufferings should blot out the remembrance of past misfortunes, and of the outcries formerly raised against the royal family. Whatever miscarriages might have given occasion to them, they have been more than atoned for since; and the nation has now an opportunity of being secured against the like in future.

"That our family has suffered exile during these fifty-seven years everybody knows. Has the nation, during that period of time, been the more happy and flourishing for it? Have you found reason to love and cherish your governors as the fathers of the people of Great Britain and Ireland? Has a family, upon whom a faction unlawfully bestowed the diadem of a rightful prince, retained a due sense of so great a trust and favour? Have you found more humanity and condescension in those who were not born to a crown, than in my royal forefathers? Have their ears been open to the cries of the people? Have they, or do they consider only the interest of these nations? Have you reaped any other benefit from them than an immense load of debt? If I am answered in the affirmative, why has their government been so often railed at in all your public assemblies? Why has the nation been so long crying out in vain for redress against the abuse of Parliaments, upon account of their long duration, the multitude of placemen, which occasions their venality, the introduction of penal laws, and, in general, against the miserable situation of the kingdom at home and abroad? All these, and many more inconveniences, must now be removed, unless the people of Great Britain be already so far corrupted that they will not accept of freedom when offered to them, seeing the King, on his restoration, will refuse nothing that a free Parliament can ask for the security of the religion, laws, and liberty of his people.

"It is now time to conclude; and I shall do it with this reflection. Civil wars are ever attended

with rancour and ill-will, which party rage never
fails to produce in the minds of those whom different interests, principles, or views, set in opposition to one another. I, therefore, earnestly require
it of my friends to give as little loose as possible to
such passions: this will prove the most effectual
means to prevent the same in the enemies of my
royal cause. And this my declaration will vindicate
to all posterity the nobleness of my undertaking,
and the generosity of my intentions."

There was much truth in the open charges
preferred in this declaration against the existing
government. The sovereigns of the house of
Hanover had always shown a marked predilec-
tion for their Continental possessions, and had
proportionally neglected the affairs of Britain.
Under Walpole's administration the imperial
Parliament had degenerated from an independent
assembly to a junta of placemen, and the most
flagitious system of bribery was openly practised
and avowed. It was not without reason that
Charles contrasted the state of the nation then,
with its position when under the rule of the legiti-
mate family; and had there not been a strong,
though, I think, unreasonable suspicion in the
minds of many, that his success would be the
prelude to a vigorous attack upon the established
religions of the country, and that he would be
inclined to follow out in this respect the fatal
policy of his grandfather, Charles would in all
probability have received a more active and general
support than was accorded to him. The zeal with
which the Episcopalian party in Scotland espoused
his cause, naturally gave rise to the idea that the
attempt of the Prince was of evil omen to Pres-
bytery; and the settlement of the Church upon
its present footing was yet so recent, that the sores
of the old feud were still festering and green. The
Established clergy, therefore, were, nearly to a man,
opposed to his pretensions; and one minister of
Edinburgh, at the time when the Highland host

was in possession of the city, had the courage to
conclude his prayer nearly in the following terms
—"Bless the king; Thou knows what king I
mean—may his crown long sit easy on his head.
And as to this young man who has come among
us to seek an earthly crown, we beseech Thee in
mercy to take him to Thyself, and give him a crown
of glory!"   At the same time, it is very curious to
observe, that the most violent sect of Presbyterians,
who might be considered as the representatives
of the extreme Cameronian principle, and who
had early seceded from the Church, and bitterly
opposed the union of the kingdoms, were not
indisposed, on certain terms, to coalesce with the
Jacobites.   It is hardly possible to understand the
motives which actuated these men, who appear
to have regarded each successive government as
equally obnoxious.   Some writers go the length of
averring that, in 1688, a negotiation was opened by
one section of the Covenanters with Lord Dundee,
with the object of resistance to the usurpation of
William of Orange, and that the project was
frustrated only by the death of that heroic nobleman.   Sir Walter Scott—a great authority—seems
to have been convinced that such was the case;
but, in the absence of direct proof, I can hardly
credit it.   It is perfectly well known that a con-
spiracy was formed by a certain section of the
Cameronian party to assassinate Lords Dundee
and Dunfermline whilst in attendance at the
meeting of Estates; and, although the recognition
of William as king might not have been palatable
to others who held the same opinions, it would be
a strange thing if they had so suddenly resolved to
assist Dundee in his efforts for the exiled family.
But the political changes in Scotland, more
especially the union, seem to have inspired some
of these men with a spirit of disaffection to the
government; for, according to Mr. Chambers, the
most rigid sect of Presbyterians had, since the
revolution, expressed a strong desire to coalesce

with the Jacobites, with the hope, in case the
house of Stuart were restored, to obtain what
they called a covenanted king.   Of this sect one
thousand had assembled in Dumfriesshire at the
first intelligence of the insurrection, bearing arms
and colours, and supposed to contemplate a junc-
tion with the Chevalier.   But these religionists
were now almost as violently distinct from the
Established Church of Scotland as ever they had
been from those of England and Rome, and had
long ceased to play a prominent part in the national
disputes.   The Established clergy, and the greater
part of their congregations, were averse to Charles
upon considerations perfectly moderate, at the same
time not easy to be shaken.

On commencing his march into England, Charles
found himself at the head of an army of between
five thousand and six thousand men, which force
was considered strong enough, with the augmen-
tations it might receive on the way, to effect the
occupation of London.   Had the English Jacobites
performed their part with the same zeal as the
Scots, it is more than probable that the attempt
would have been crowned with success.   As it was,
the Prince succeeded in reducing the strong forti-
fied town of Carlisle, and in marching, without
opposition, through the heart of England, as far as
Derby, within one hundred miles of the metropolis.
But here his better genius deserted him.   Discord
had crept into his councils ; for some of the chiefs
became seriously alarmed at finding that the gentry
of England were not prepared to join the expedition, but preferred remaining at home inactive
spectators of the contest.   Except at Manchester,
they had received few or no recruits.   No tidings
had reached them from Wales, a country supposed
to be devoted to the cause of King James, whilst it
was well known that a large force was already in
arms to oppose the clans.   Mr. Chambers gives us
the following details :—" At a council of war held
on the morning of the 5th December, Lord George

Murray and the other members gave it as their unanimous opinion that the army ought to return to Scotland. Lord George pointed out that they were about to be environed by three armies, amounting collectively to about thirty thousand men, while their own forces were not above five thousand, if so many. Supposing an unsuccessful engagement with any of these armies, it could not be expected that one man would escape, for the militia would beset every road. The Prince, if not slain in the battle, must fall into the enemy's hands : the whole world would blame them as fools for running into such a risk. Charles answered, that he regarded not his own danger. He pressed, with all the force of argument, to go forward. He did not doubt, he said, that the justice of his cause would prevail. He was hopeful that there might be a defection in the enemy s army, and that many would declare for him. He was so very bent on putting all to the risk, that the Duke of Perth was for it, since his Royal Highness was. At last he proposed going to Wales instead of returning to Carlisle ; but every other officer declared his opinion for a retreat. These are nearly the words of Lord George Murray. We are elsewhere told that the Prince condescended to use entreaties to induce his adherents to alter their resolution. ' Rather than go back,' he said, ' I would wish to be twenty feet under ground !' His chagrin, when he found his councillors obdurate, was beyond all bounds. The council broke up, on the understanding that the retreat was to commence next morning, Lord George volunteering to take the place of honour in the rear, provided only that he should not be troubled with the baggage."

This resolution was received by the army with marks of unequivocal vexation. Retreat, in their estimation, was little less than overthrow ; and it was most galling to find that, after all their labours, hazards, and toils, they were doomed to disappointment at the very moment when the prize

seemed ready for their grasp.   That the movement
was an injudicious one is, I think, obvious.   We
are told, upon good authority, "that the very bold-
ness of the Prince's onward movement, especially
taken into connection with the expected descent
from France, had at length disposed the English
Jacobites to come out ; and many were just on the
point of declaring themselves, and marching to
join his army, when the retreat from Derby was
determined on.   A Mr. Barry arrived in Derby
two days after the Prince left it, with a message
from Sir Watkin William Wynne and Lord Barry-
more, to assure him, in the names of many friends
of the cause, that they were ready to join him in
what manner he pleased, either in the capital, or
every one to rise in his own county.   I have likewise been assured that many of the Welsh gentry
had actually left their homes, and were on the way
to join Charles, when intelligence of his retreat at
once sent them all back peaceably, convinced that
it was now too late to contribute their assistance.
These men, from the power they had over their
tenantry, could have added materially to his
military force.   In fact, from all that appears, we
must conclude that the insurgents had a very
considerable chance of success from an onward
movement—also, no doubt, a chance of destruction,
and yet not worse than what ultimately befell
many of them—while a retreat broke in a moment
the spell which their gallantry had conjured up,
and gave the enemy a great advantage over them."

One victory more was accorded to Prince Charles,
before his final overthrow.   After successfully conducting his retreat to Scotland, occupying Glasgow,
and strengthening his army by the accession of
new recruits, he gave battle to the royal forces
under General Hawley at Falkirk, and, as at
Preston, drove them from the field.   The parties
were on this occasion fairly matched, there being
about eight thousand men engaged on either side.
The action was short ; and, though not so decisive

as the former one, gave great confidence to the insurgents. It has been thus picturesquely portrayed by the historian of the enterprise: "Some individuals, who beheld the battle from the steeple of Falkirk, used to describe these, its main events, as occupying a surprisingly brief space of time. They first saw the English army enter the misty and storm-covered muir at the top of the hill; then saw the dull atmosphere thickened by a fast-rolling smoke, and heard the pealing sounds of the discharge; immediately after, they beheld the discomfited troops burst wildly from the cloud in which they had been involved, and rush, in far-spread disorder, over the face of the hill. From the commencement of what they styled 'the *break* of the battle,' there did not intervene more than ten minutes—so soon may an efficient body of men become, by one transient emotion of cowardice, a feeble and contemptible rabble.

· "The rout would have been total, but for the three out-flanking regiments. These not having been opposed by any of the clans, having a ravine in front, and deriving some support from a small body of dragoons, stood their ground under the command of General Huske and Brigadier Cholmondley. When the Highlanders went past in pursuit, they received a volley from this part of the English army, which brought them to a pause, and caused them to draw back to their former ground, their impression being that some ambuscade was intended. This saved the English army from destruction. A pause took place, during which the bulk of the English infantry got back to Falkirk. It was not until Lord George Murray brought up the second line of his wing and the pickets, with some others on the other wing, that General Huske drew off his party, which he did in good order."

The seat of war was now removed to the North. The month of April 1746 found Prince Charles in possession of Inverness, with an army sorely

F

dwindled in numbers, and in great want of neces-
saries and provisions. Many of the Highlanders
had retired for the winter to their native glens,
and had not yet rejoined the standard. The
Duke of Cumberland, who now commanded the
English army, with a reputation not diminished
by the unfortunate issue of Fontenoy, was at the
head of a large body of tried and disciplined
troops, in the best condition, and supported by
the powerful arm of artillery. He effected the
passage of the Spey, a large and rapid river which
intersects the Highlands, without encountering any
opposition, and on the 15th of the month had
arrived at Nairn, about nine miles distant from
the position occupied by his kinsman and opponent. His superiority in point of strength was
so great that the boldest of the insurgent chiefs
hesitated as to the policy of giving immediate
battle; and nothing but the desire of covering
Inverness prevented the council from recommenc-
ing a further retreat into the mountains, where
they could not have been easily followed, and
where they were certain to have met with reinforcements. As to the Prince, his confidence in
the prowess of the Highlanders was so unbounded,
that, even with such odds against him, he would
not listen to a proposal for delay.

There yet remained, says Mr. Chambers, before
playing the great stake of a pitched battle, one
chance of success, by the irregular mode of warfare to which the army was accustomed; and
Charles resolved to put it to trial. This was a
night-attack upon the camp of the Duke of
Cumberland. He rightly argued, that if his
men could approach without being discovered,
and make a simultaneous attack in more than
one place, the royal forces, then probably either
engaged in drinking their commander's health
(the 15th happened to be the anniversary of the
Duke's birthday, and was celebrated as such by
his army), or sleeping off the effects of the de-

bauch, must be completely surprised and cut to pieces, or at least effectually routed. The time appointed for setting out upon the march was eight in the evening, when daylight should have completely disappeared; and, in the meantime, great pains were taken to conceal the secret from the army.

This resolution was entered into at three in the afternoon, and orders were given to collect the men who had gone off in search of provisions. The officers dispersed themselves to Inverness and other places, and besought the stragglers to repair to the muir. But, under the influence of hunger, they told their commanders to shoot them if they pleased, rather than compel them to starve any longer. Charles had previously declared, with his characteristic fervour, that though only a thousand of his men should accompany him, he would lead them on to the attack; and he was not now intimidated when he saw twice that number ready to assist in the enterprise; though some of his officers would willingly have made this deficiency of troops an excuse for abandoning what they esteemed at best a hazardous expedition. Having given out for watchword the name of his father, he embraced Lord George Murray, who was to command the foremost column, and putting himself at the head of that which followed, gave the order to march.

· The attempt proved peculiarly unfortunate, and, from the fatigue which it occasioned to the Highlanders, contributed in a great degree towards the disaster of the following day. The night chanced to be uncommonly dark, and as it was well known that Cumberland had stationed spies on the principal roads, it became necessary to select a devious route, in order to effect a surprise. The columns, proceeding over broken and irregular ground, soon became scattered and dislocated: no exertions of the officers could keep the men together, so that Lord George Murray at two o'clock found that he was still distant three miles from the hostile camp, and that there were no hopes of commencing the attack before the break of day, when they would be open to the observation of the enemy. Under these circumstances a retreat was commenced ; and the scheme, which at one time seemed to hold out every probability of success, was abandoned.

"The Highlanders returned, fatigued and disconsolate, to their former position, about seven in the morning, when they immediately addressed themselves to sleep, or went away in search of provisions. So scarce was food at this critical juncture, that the Prince himself, on retiring to Culloden House, could obtain no better refreshment than a little bread and whisky. He felt the utmost anxiety regarding his men, among whom the pangs of hunger, upon bodies exhausted by fatigue, must have been working effects most unpromising to his success ; and he gave orders, before seeking any repose, that the whole country should now be mercilessly ransacked for the means of refreshment. His orders were not without effect. Considerable supplies were procured, and subjected to the cook's art at Inverness ; but the poor famished clansmen were destined never to taste these provisions, the hour of battle arriving before they were prepared."

About eleven in the forenoon, the troops of Cumberland were observed upon the eastern extremity of the wide muir of Culloden, and preparations were instantly made for the coming battle. The army had been strengthened that morning by the arrival of the Keppoch Macdonalds and a party of the Frasers ; but even with these reinforcements the whole available force which the Prince could muster was about five thousand men, to oppose at fearful odds an enemy twice as numerous, and heavily supported by artillery. Fortune on this day seemed to have deserted the Prince altogether. In drawing out the line of

battle, a most unlucky arrangement was made by
O'Sullivan, who acted as adjutant, whereby the
Macdonald regiments were removed from the right
wing—the place which the great clan Colla has
been privileged to hold in Scottish array ever since
the auspicious battle of Bannockburn.   To those
who are not acquainted with the peculiar temper
and spirit of the Highlanders, and their punctilio
upon points of honour and precedence, the question
of arrangement will naturally appear a matter
of little importance.   But it was not so felt by
the Macdonalds, who considered their change of
position as a positive degradation, and who further
looked upon it as an evil omen to the success
of the battle.   The results of this mistake will be
explained immediately.

Just before the commencement of the action, the
weather, which had hitherto been fair and sunny,
became overcast, and a heavy blast of rain and
sleet beat directly in the faces of the Highlanders.
The English artillery then began to play upon
them, and, being admirably served, every discharge told with fearful effect upon the ranks.
The chief object of either party at the battle of
Culloden seems to have been to force its opponent
to leave his position, and to commence the attack.
Cumberland, finding that his artillery was doing
such execution, had no occasion to move; and
Charles appears to have committed a great error
in abandoning a mode of warfare which was
peculiarly suited for his troops, and which, on
two previous occasions, had proved eminently
successful.   Had he at once ordered a general
charge, and attempted to silence the guns, the
issue of the day might have been otherwise : but
his unfortunate star prevailed.

"It was not," says Mr. Chambers, "till the
cannonade had continued nearly half an hour,
and the Highlanders had seen many of their
kindred stretched upon the heath, that Charles
at last gave way to the necessity of ordering a

charge. The aide-de-camp intrusted to carry his
message to the lieutenant-general—a youth of the
name of Maclachlan—was killed by a cannon-ball
before he reached the first line ; but the general
sentiment of the army, as reported to Lord George
Murray, supplied the want, and that general took
it upon him to order an attack without Charles's
permission having been communicated.

"Lord George had scarcely determined upon
ordering a general movement, when the Macin-
toshes, a brave and devoted clan, though not
before engaged in action, unable any longer to
brook the unavenged slaughter made by the
cannon, broke from the centre of the line, and
rushed forward through smoke and snow to mingle
with the enemy. The Athole men, Camerons,
Stuarts, Frasers, and Macleans also went on, Lord
George Murray heading them with that rash bravery
befitting the commander of such forces. Thus, in
the course of one or two minutes, the charge was
general along the whole line, except at the left
extremity, where the Macdonalds, dissatisfied with
their position, hesitated to engage.

"The action and event of the onset were, throughout, quite as dreadful as the mental emotion which
urged it. Notwithstanding that the three files of
the front line of English poured forth their incessant
fire of musketry—notwithstanding that the cannon,
now loaded with grapeshot, swept the field as with
a hailstorm—notwithstanding the flank fire of
Wolfe's regiment—onward, onward went the headlong Highlanders, flinging themselves into rather
than rushing upon, the lines of the enemy, which,
indeed, they did not see for smoke, till involved
among the weapons. All that courage, all that
despair could do, was done. It was a moment of
dreadful and agonising suspense, but only a moment
—for the whirlwind does not reap the forest with
greater rapidity than the Highlanders cleared the
line. Nevertheless, almost every man in their front
rank, chief and gentleman, fell before the deadly

weapons which they had braved; and, although
the enemy gave way, it was not till every bayonet
was bent and bloody with the strife.

"When the first line had thus been swept aside,
the assailants continued their impetuous advance
till they came near the second, when, being almost
annihilated by a profuse and well-directed fire,
the shattered remains of what had been before a
numerous and confident force began to give way.
Still a few rushed on, resolved rather to die than
forfeit their well-acquired and dearly-estimated
honour. They rushed on; but not a man ever
came in contact with the enemy. The last survivor
perished as he reached the points of the bayonets."

Some idea of the determination displayed by the
Highlanders in this terrific charge may be gathered
from the fact that, in one part of the field, their
bodies were afterwards found in layers of three
and four deep. The slaughter was fearful, for,
out of the five regiments which charged the
English, almost all the leaders and men in the
front rank were killed. So shaken was the English
line, that, had the Macdonald regiments, well-
known to yield in valour to none of the clans,
come up, the fortune of the day might have been
altered. But they never made an onset. Smart-
ing and sullen at the affront which they conceived
to have been put upon their name, they bore the
fire of the English regiments without flinching,
and gave way to their rage by hewing at the
heather with their swords. In vain their chiefs
exhorted them to go forward: even at that terrible
moment the pride of clanship prevailed. "My
God!" cried Macdonald of Keppoch, "has it
come to this, that the children of my tribe have
forsaken me!" and he rushed forward alone, sword
in hand, with the devotion of an ancient hero, and
fell pierced with bullets.

The Lowland and foreign troops which formed
the second line were powerless to retrieve the
disaster. All was over. The rout became general,

and the Prince was forced from the field, which
he would not quit, until dragged from it by his
immediate bodyguard.

. Such was the last battle, the result of civil war,
which has been fought on British soil. Those who
were defeated have acquired as much glory from
it as the conquerors—and even more, for never
was a conquest sullied by such deeds of deliberate
cruelty as were perpetrated upon the survivors of
the battle of Culloden. It is not, however, the
object of the present paper to recount these, or
even the romantic history or hairbreadth escapes
of the Prince, whilst wandering on the mainland
and through the Hebrides. Although a reward
of thirty thousand pounds—an immense sum for
the period—was set upon his head—although his
secret was known to hundreds of persons in every
walk of life, and even to the beggar and the outlaw
—not one attempted to betray him. Not one of
all his followers, in the midst of the misery which
overtook them, regretted having drawn the sword
in his cause, or would not again have gladly imperilled their lives for the sake of their beloved
Chevalier. "He went," says Lord Mahon, "but
not with him departed his remembrance from the
Highlanders. For years and years did his name
continue enshrined in their hearts and familiar to
their tongues, their plaintive ditties resounding
with his exploits and inviting his return. Again,
in these strains, do they declare themselves ready
to risk life and fortune for his cause; and even
maternal fondness—the strongest, perhaps, of all
human feelings—yields to the passionate devotion
to Prince Charlie."

The subsequent life of the Prince is a story of
melancholy interest. We find him at first received
in France with all the honours due to one who,
though unfortunate, had exhibited a heroism rarely
equalled and never surpassed: gradually he was
neglected and slighted, as one of a doomed and
unhappy race, whom no human exertion could

avail to elevate to their former seat of power; and finally, when his presence in France became an obstacle to the conclusion of peace, he was violently arrested and conveyed out of the kingdom. There can be little doubt that continued misfortune and disappointment had begun very early to impair his noble mind. For long periods he was a wanderer, lost sight of by his friends and even by his father and brother. There are fragments of his writing extant which show how poignantly he felt the cruelty of his fortune. " De vivre et pas vivre est beaucoup plus que de mourir ! " And again, writing to his father's secretary, eight years after Culloden, he says : — " I am grieved that our master should think that my silence was either neglect or want of duty; but, in reality, my situation is such that I have nothing to say but imprecations against the fatality of being born in such a detestable age." An unhappy and uncongenial marriage tended still more to embitter his existence; and if at last he yielded to frailties, which inevitably insure degradation, it must be remembered that his lot had been one to which few men have ever been exposed, and the magnitude of his sufferings may fairly be admitted as some palliation for his weakness.

To the last, his heart was with Scotland. The following anecdote was related by his brother, Cardinal York, to Bishop Walker, the late Primus of the Episcopal Church of Scotland : — " Mr. Greathead, a personal friend of Mr. Fox, succeeded, when at Rome in 1782 or 1783, in obtaining an interview with Charles Edward ; and, being alone with him for some time, studiously led the conversation to his enterprise in Scotland, and to the occurrences which succeeded the failure of that attempt. The Prince manifested some reluctance to enter upon these topics, appearing at the same time to undergo so much mental suffering, that his guest regretted the freedom he had used in calling up the remembrance of his misfortunes. At length,

however, the Prince seemed to shake off the load
which oppressed him ; his eye brightened, his face
assumed unwonted animation, and he entered
upon the narrative of his Scottish campaigns with
a distinct but somewhat vehement energy of manner—recounted his marches, his battles, his vic-
tories, his retreats, and his defeats—detailed his
hairbreadth escapes in the Western Isles, the in-
violable and devoted attachment of his Highland
friends, and at length proceeded to allude to the
terrible penalties with which the chiefs among
them had been visited.   But here the tide of
emotion rose too high to allow him to go on—his
voice faltered, his eyes became fixed, and he fell
convulsed on the floor.   The noise brought into
his room his daughter, the Duchess of Albany,
who happened to be in an adjoining apartment.
'Sir,' she exclaimed, 'what is this? You have
been speaking to my father about Scotland and
the Highlanders ! No one dares to mention those
subjects in his presence.' "

He died on the 30th of January 1788, in the
arms of the Master of Nairn.   The monument
erected to him, his father, and brother, in St.
Peter's, by desire of George IV., was perhaps the
most graceful tribute ever paid by royalty to misfortune—REGIO CINERI PIETAS REGIA.

CHARLES EDWARD AT VERSAILLES.

TAKE away that star and garter—
   Hide them from my aching sight:
Neither king nor prince shall tempt me
   From my lonely room this night;
Fitting for the throneless exile
   Is the atmosphere of pall,
And the gusty winds that shiver
   'Neath the tapestry on the wall.
When the taper faintly dwindles
   Like the pulse within the vein,
That to gay and merry measure
   Ne'er may hope to bound again,
Let the shadows gather round me
   While I sit in silence here,
Broken-hearted, as an orphan
   Watching by his father's bier.
Let me hold my still communion
   Far from every earthly sound—
Day of penance—day of passion—
   Ever, as the year comes round:
Fatal day, whereon the latest
   Die was cast for me and mine—
Cruel day, that quelled the fortunes
   Of the hapless Stuart line!
Phantom-like, as in a mirror,
   Rise the griesly scenes of death—
There before me, in its wildness,
   . Stretches bare Culloden's heath:
There the broken clans are scattered,
   Gaunt as wolves, and famine-eyed,
Hunger gnawing at their vitals,

Hope abandoned, all but pride—
Pride—and that supreme devotion
  Which the Southron never knew,
And the hatred, deeply rankling,
  'Gainst the Hanoverian crew.
Oh, my God! are these the remnants,
  These the wrecks of the array,
That around the royal standard
  Gathered on the glorious day,
When, in deep Glenfinnan's valley,
  Thousands, on their bended knees,
Saw once more that stately ensign
  Waving in the northern breeze,
When the noble Tullibardine
  Stood beneath its weltering fold,
With the Ruddy Lion ramping
  In the field of tressured gold!
When the mighty heart of Scotland,
  All too big to slumber more,
Burst in wrath and exultation,
  Like a huge volcano's roar!
There they stand, the battered columns,
  Underneath the murky sky,
In the hush of desperation,
  Not to conquer but to die.
Hark! the bagpipe's fitful wailing:
  Not the pibroch loud and shrill,
That, with hope of bloody banquet,
  Lured the ravens from the hill,
But a dirge both low and solemn,
  Fit for ears of dying men,
Marshalled for their latest battle,
  Never more to fight again.
Madness—madness! Why this shrinking?
  Were we less inured to war
When our reapers swept the harvest
  From the field of red Dunbar?
Bring my horse, and blow the trumpet!
  Call the riders of Fitz-James:
Let Lord Lewis head the column!
  Valiant chiefs of mighty names—

Trusty Keppoch! stout Glengarry!
  Gallant Gordon! wise Locheill!—
Bid the clansmen hold together,
  Fast, and fell, and firm as steel.
Elcho! never look so gloomy—
  What avails a saddened brow?
Heart, man, heart!—We need it sorely,
  Never half so much as now.
Had we but a thousand troopers,
  Had we but a thousand more!
Noble Perth, I hear them coming!—
  Hark! the English cannons' roar.
God! how awful sounds that volley,
  Bellowing through the mist and rain!
Was not that the Highland slogan?
  Let me hear that shout again!
Oh, for prophet eyes to witness
  How the desperate battle goes!
Cumberland! I would not fear thee,
  Could my Camerons see their foes.
Sound, I say, the charge at venture—
  'Tis not naked steel we fear;
Better perish in the *mêlée*
  Than be shot like driven deer!
Hold! the mist begins to scatter!
  There in front 'tis rent asunder,
And the cloudy bastion crumbles
  Underneath the deafening thunder;
There I see the scarlet gleaming!
  Now, Macdonald,—now or never!—
Woe is me, the clans are broken!
  Father, thou art lost for ever!
Chief and vassal, lord and yeoman,
  There they lie in heaps together,
Smitten by the deadly volley,
  Rolled in blood upon the heather;
And the Hanoverian horsemen,
  Fiercely riding to and fro,
Deal their murderous strokes at random.—

  Ah, my God? where am I now?

Will that baleful vision never
    Vanish from my aching sight?
Must those scenes and sounds of terror
    Haunt me still by day and night?
Yea, the earth hath no oblivion
    For the noblest chance it gave,
None, save in its latest refuge—
    Seek it only in the grave!
Love may die, and hatred slumber,
    And their memory will decay,
As the watered garden recks not
    Of the drought of yesterday;
But the dream of power once broken
    What shall give repose again?
What shall charm the serpent-furies
    Coiled around the maddening brain?
What kind draught can nature offer
    Strong enough to lull their sting?
Better to be born a peasant
    Than to live an exiled king!
Oh, these years of bitter anguish!—
    What is life to such as me,
With my very heart as palsied
    As a wasted cripple's knee!
Suppliant-like for alms depending
    On a false and foreign court,
Jostled by the flouting nobles,
    Half their pity, half their sport.
Forced to hold a place in pageant,
    Like a royal prize of war,
Walking with dejected features
    Close behind his victor's car,
Styled an equal—deemed a servant—
    Fed with hopes of future gain—
Worse by far is fancied freedom
    Than the captive's clanking chain!
Could I change this gilded bondage
    Even for the dusky tower,
Whence King James beheld his lady
    Sitting in the castle bower;
Birds around her sweetly singing,

Fluttering on the kindling spray,
And the comely garden glowing
  In the light of rosy May.
Love descended to the window—
  Love removed the bolt and bar—
Love was warder to the lovers
  From the dawn to even-star.
Wherefore, Love, didst thou betray me?
  Where is now the tender glance?
Where the meaning looks once lavished
  By the dark-eyed Maid of France?
Where the words of hope she whispered,
  When around my neck she threw
That same scarf of broidered tissue,
  Bade me wear it and be true—
Bade me send it as a token
  When my banner waved once more
On the castled Keep of London,
  Where my fathers' waved before?
And I went and did not conquer—
  But I brought it back again—
Brought it back from storm and battle—
  Brought it back without a stain ;
And once more I knelt before her,
  And I laid it at her feet,
Saying, "Wilt thou own it, Princess?
  There at least is no defeat!"
Scornfully she looked upon me
  With a measured eye and cold—
Scornfully she viewed the token,
  Though her fingers wrought the gold;
And she answered, faintly flushing,
  "Hast thou kept it, then, so long?
Worthy matter for a minstrel
  To be told in knightly song!
Worthy of a bold Provençal,
  Pacing through the peaceful plain,
Singing of his lady's favour,
  Boasting of her silken chain,
Yet scarce worthy of a warrior
  Sent to wrestle for a crown.

Is this all that thou hast brought me
  From thy fields of high renown?
Is this all the trophy carried
  From the lands where thou hast been?
It was broidered by a Princess,
  Canst thou give it to a Queen?"
Woman's love is writ in water!
  Woman's faith is traced in sand!
Backwards—backwards let me wander
  To the noble northern land:
Let me feel the breezes blowing
  Fresh along the mountain-side;
Let me see the purple heather,
  Let me hear the thundering tide,
Be it hoarse as Corrievreckan
  Spouting when the storm is high—
Give me but one hour of Scotland—
  Let me see it ere I die!
Oh, my heart is sick and heavy—
  Southern gales are not for me;
Though the glens are white with winter,
  Place me there, and set me free;
Give me back my trusty comrades—
  Give me back my Highland maid—
Nowhere beats the heart so kindly
  As beneath the tartan plaid!
Flora! when thou wert beside me,
  In the wilds of far Kintail—
When the cavern gave us shelter
  From the blinding sleet and hail—
When we lurked within the thicket,
  And, beneath the waning moon,
Saw the sentry's bayonet glimmer,
  Heard him chaunt his listless tune—
When the howling storm o'ertook us,
  Drifting down the island's lee,
And our crazy bark was whirling
  Like a nutshell on the sea—
When the nights were dark and dreary,
  And amidst the fern we lay,
Faint and foodless, sore with travel,

Waiting for the streaks of day ;
When thou wert an angel to me,
   Watching my exhausted sleep—
Never didst thou hear me murmur—
   Couldst thou see how now I weep !
Bitter tears and sobs of anguish,
   Unavailing though they be :
Oh, the brave—the brave and noble—
   That have died in vain for me !

NOTES TO "CHARLES EDWARD AT VERSAILLES."

Could I change this gilded bondage
Even for the dusky tower
Whence King James beheld his lady
Sitting in the castle bower.—P. 134.

James I. of Scotland, one of the most accomplished kings that ever sate upon a throne, is the person here indicated. His history is a very strange and romantic one. He was son of Robert III., and immediate younger brother of that unhappy Duke of Rothesay who was murdered at Falkland. His father, apprehensive of the designs and treachery of Albany, had determined to remove him, when a mere boy, for a season from Scotland; and as France was then considered the best school for the education of one so important from his high position, it was resolved to send him thither, under the care of the Earl of Orkney, and Fleming of Cumbernauld. He accordingly embarked at North Berwick, with little escort—as there was a truce for the time between England and Scotland; and they were under no apprehension of meeting with any vessels, save those of the former nation. Notwithstanding this, the ship which carried the Prince was captured by an armed merchantman, and carried to London, where Henry IV., the usurping Bolingbroke, utterly regardless of treaties, committed him and his attendants to the Tower.

" In vain," says Mr. Tytler, " did the guardians of the young Prince remonstrate against this cruelty, or present to Henry a letter from the King his father, which, with much simplicity, recommended him to the kindness of the English monarch, should he find it necessary to land in his dominions. In vain did they represent that the mission to France was perfectly pacific, and its only object the education of the Prince at the French court. Henry merely answered by a poor witticism, declaring that he himself knew the French language indifferently well, and that his father could not have sent him to a better master. So flagrant a breach of the law of nations, as the seizure and imprisonment of the heir-apparent, during the time of truce, would have called for the most violent remonstrances from any government, except that of Albany. But to this usurper of the supreme power, the capture of the Prince was the most grateful event which could have happened ; and to detain him in captivity became, from this moment, one of the principal objects of his future life ; we are not to wonder, then, that the conduct of Henry not only drew forth no indignation from the governor, but was not even followed by any request that the Prince should be set at liberty.

"The aged King, already worn out by infirmity, and now broken by disappointment and sorrow, did not long survive the captivity of his son. It is said the melancholy news were brought him as he was sitting down to supper in his palace of Rothesay in Bute, and that the effect was such upon his affectionate but feeble spirit, that he drooped from that day forward, refused all sustenance, and died soon after of a broken heart."

James was finally incarcerated in Windsor Castle, where he endured an imprisonment of nineteen years. Henry, though he had not hesitated to commit a heinous breach of faith, was not so cruel as to neglect the education of his captive. The young King was supplied with the best masters ; and gradually became an adept in all the accom-

plishments of the age. He is a singular exception
from the rule which maintains that monarchs are
indifferent authors. As a poet, he is entitled to
a very high rank indeed, being, I think, in point
of sweetness and melody of verse, not much
inferior to Chaucer. From the window of his
chamber in the Tower, he had often seen a
young lady, of great beauty and grace, walking
in the garden ; and the admiration which at once
possessed him soon ripened into love. This was
Lady Jane Beaufort, daughter of the Earl of
Somerset and niece of Henry IV., and who afterwards became his queen. How he loved and how
he wooed her is told in his own beautiful poem of
" The King's Quhair," of which the following are
a few stanzas :—

" Now there was made, fast by the towris wall,
　A garden fair ; and in the corners set
　An arbour green, with wandis long and small
　Railed about, and so with trees set
　Was all the place, and hawthorn hedges knet,
　That lyf was none walking there forbye,
　That might within scarce any wight espy.

So thick the boughis and the leavis greene
　Beshaded all the alleys that there were,
　And mids of every arbour might be seen
　The sharpe, greene, sweete juniper,
　Growing so fair, with branches here and there,
　That, as it seemed to a lyf without,
　The boughis spread the arbour all about.

And on the smalle greene twistis sat
　The little sweete nightingale, and sung
　So loud and clear the hymnis consecrat
　Of lovis use, now soft, now loud among,
　That all the gardens and the wallis rung
　Right of their song.

And therewith cast I down mine eyes again,
　Where as I saw, walking under the tower,
　Full secretly, now comen here to plain,
　The fairest or the freshest younge flower
　That e'er I saw, methought, before that hour :

For which sudden abate, anon astart
The blood of all my body to my heart.

And though I stood abasit for a lite,
No wonder was ; for why? my wittis all
Were so o'ercome with pleasance and delight—
Only through letting of my eyen fall—
That suddenly my heart became her thrall
For ever of free will, for of menace
There was no token in her sweete face."

Wherefore, Love, didst thou betray me?
Where is now the tender glance?
Where the meaning looks once lavished
By the dark-eyed Maid of France?—P. 135.

There appears to be no doubt that Prince Charles was deeply attached to one of the princesses of the royal family of France. In the interesting collection called "Jacobite Memoirs," compiled by Mr. Chambers from the voluminous MSS. of Bishop Forbes, we find the following passage from the narrative of Donald Macleod, who acted as a guide to the wanderer whilst traversing the Hebrides :—"When Donald was asked, if ever the Prince used to give any particular toast, when they were taking a cup of cold water, or the like ; he said that the Prince very often drank to the Black Eye—by which, said Donald, he meant the second daughter of France, and I never heard him name any particular health but that alone. When he spoke of that lady—which he did frequently—he appeared to be more than ordinarily well pleased."

✤

THE OLD SCOTTISH CAVALIER.

THE " gentle Locheill " may be considered as the
pattern of a Highland Chief. Others who headed
the insurrection may have been actuated by motives
of personal ambition, and by a desire for aggran-
disement ; but no such charge can be made against
the generous and devoted Cameron. He was, as
we have already seen, the first who attempted to
dissuade the Prince from embarking in an enterprise which be conscientiously believed to be desperate ; but, having failed in doing so, he nobly
stood firm to the cause which his conscience vindi-
cated as just, and cheerfully imperilled his life,
and sacrificed his fortune, at the bidding of his
master. There was no one, even among those
who espoused the other side, in Scotland, who
did not commiserate the misfortunes of this truly
excellent man, whose humanity was not less conspicuous than bis valour throughout the civil war,
and who died in exile of a broken heart.

Perhaps the best type of the Lowland Cavalier
of that period, may be found in the person of
Alexander Forbes, Lord Pitsligo, a nobleman
whose conscientious views impelled him to take
a different side from that adopted by the greater
part of his house and name. Lord Forbes, the
head of this very ancient and honourable family,
was one of the first Scottish noblemen who declared for King William. Lord Pitsligo, on the
contrary, having been educated abroad, and early
introduced to the circle at Saint Germains, con-

ceived a deep personal attachment to the members of the exiled line. He was anything but an enthusiast, as his philosophical and religious writings, well worthy of a perusal, will show. He was the intimate friend of Fénélon, and throughout his whole life was remarkable rather for his piety and virtue, than for keenness in political dispute.

After his return from France, Lord Pitsligo took his seat in the Scottish Parliament, and his parliamentary career has thus been characterised by a former writer.* "Here it is no discredit either to his head or heart to say, that, obliged to become a member of one of the contending factions of the time, he adopted that which had for its object the independence of Scotland, and restoration of the ancient race of monarchs. The advantages which were in future to arise from the great measure of a national union were so hidden by the mists of prejudice, that it cannot be wondered at if Lord Pitsligo, like many a high-spirited man, saw nothing but disgrace in a measure forced on by such corrupt means, and calling in its commencement for such mortifying national sacrifices. The English nation, indeed, with a narrow, yet not unnatural, view of their own interest, took such pains to encumber and restrict the Scottish commercial privileges, that it was not till the best part of a century after the event that the inestimable fruits of the treaty began to be felt and known. This distant period Lord Pitsligo could not foresee. He beheld his countrymen, like the Israelites of yore, led into the desert ; but his merely human eye could not foresee that, after the extinction of a whole race—after a longer pilgrimage than that of the followers of Moses—the Scottish people should at length arrive at that promised land, of which the favourers of the Union held forth so gay a prospect.

* See *Blackwood's Magazine* for May 1829.—Article "Lord Pitsligo."

"Looking upon the Act of Settlement of the Crown, and the Act of Adjuration, as unlawful, Lord Pitsligo retired to his house in the country, and threw up attendance on Parliament. Upon the death of Queen Anne he joined himself in arms with a general insurrection of the Highlanders and Jacobites, headed by his friend and relative the Earl of Mar.

"Mar, a versatile statesman and an able intriguer, had consulted his ambition rather than his talents when he assumed the command of such an enterprise. He sunk beneath the far superior genius of the Duke of Argyle; and after the undecisive battle of Sheriffmuir, the confederacy which he had formed, but was unable to direct, dissolved like a snowball, and the nobles concerned in it were fain to fly abroad. This exile was Lord Pitsligo's fate for five or six years. Part of the time he spent at the Court, if it can be called so, of the old Chevalier de Saint George, where existed all the petty feuds, chicanery, and crooked intrigues which subsist in a real scene of the same character, although the objects of the ambition which prompts such arts had no existence. Men seemed to play at being courtiers in that illusory court, as children play at being soldiers."

It would appear that Lord Pitsligo was not attainted for his share in Mar's rebellion. He returned to Scotland in 1720, and resided at his castle in Aberdeenshire, not mingling in public affairs, but gaining, through his charity, kindness, and benevolence, the respect and affection of all around him. He was sixty-seven years of age when Charles Edward landed in Scotland. The district in which the estates of Lord Pitsligo lay was essentially Jacobite, and the young cavaliers only waited for a fitting leader to take up arms in the cause. According to Mr. Home, his example was decisive of the movement of his neighbours: "So when he who was so wise and prudent declared his purpose of joining Charles, most of

G

the gentlemen in that part of the country who
favoured the Pretender's cause, put themselves
under his command, thinking they could not follow
a better or safer guide than Lord Pitsligo." His
Lordship's own account of the motives which
urged him on is peculiar :—"I was grown a little
old, and the fear of ridicule stuck to me pretty
much. I have mentioned the weightier considerations of a family, which would make the censure
still the greater, and set the more tongues agoing.
But we are pushed on, I know not how,—I
thought—I weighed—and I weighed again. If
there was any enthusiasm in it, it was of the
coldest kind ; and there was as little remorse
when the affair miscarried, as there was eagerness
at the beginning."

The writer whom I have already quoted goes on
to say—"To those friends who recalled his misfortunes of 1715, he replied gaily, 'Did you ever
know me absent at the second day of a wedding?'
meaning, I suppose, that having once contracted
an engagement, he did not feel entitled to quit it
while the contest subsisted. Being invited by the
gentlemen of the district to put himself at their
head, and having surmounted his own desires, he
had made a farewell visit at a neighbour's house,
where a little boy, a child of the family, brought
out a stool to assist the old nobleman in remount-
ing his horse. 'My little fellow,' said Lord
Pitsligo, 'this is the severest rebuke I have yet received, for presuming to go on such an expedition.'

"The die was however cast, and Lord Pitsligo
went to meet his friends at the rendezvous they
had appointed in Aberdeen. They formed a body
of well-armed cavalry, gentlemen and their servants, to the number of a hundred men. When
they were drawn up in readiness to commence the
expedition, the venerable nobleman, their leader,
moved to their front, lifted his hat, and, looking
up to heaven, pronounced, with a solemn voice,
the awful appeal,—'O Lord, Thou knowest that

our cause is just!' then added the signal for departure—'March, gentlemen!'

"Lord Pitsligo, with his followers, found Charles at Edinburgh, on 8th October 1745, a few days after the Highlanders' victory at Preston. Their arrival was hailed with enthusiasm, not only on account of the timely reinforcement, but more especially from the high character of their leader. Hamilton of Bangour, in an animated and eloquent eulogium upon Pitsligo, states that nothing could have fallen out more fortunately for the Prince than his joining them did—for it seemed as if religion, virtue, and justice were entering his camp, under the appearance of this venerable old man; and what would have given sanction to a cause of the most dubious right, could not fail to render sacred the very best."

Although so far advanced in years, he remained in arms during the whole campaign, and was treated with almost filial tenderness by the Prince. After Culloden, he became, like many more, a fugitive and an outlaw, but succeeded, like the Baron of Bradwardine, in finding a shelter upon the skirts of his own estate. Disguised as a mendicant, his secret was faithfully kept by the tenantry; and although it was more than surmised by the soldiers that he was lurking somewhere in the neighbourhood, they never were able to detect him. On one occasion he actually guided a party to a cave on the sea-shore, amidst the rough rocks of Buchan, where it was rumoured that he was lying in concealment; and on another, when overtaken by his asthma, and utterly unable to escape from an approaching patrol of soldiers, he sat down by the wayside, and acted his assumed character so well, that a good-natured fellow not only gave him alms, but condoled with him on the violence of his complaint.

For ten years he remained concealed, but in the meantime both title and estate were forfeited by attainder. His last escape was so very remarkable, that I may be pardoned for giving it in the language of the author of his memoirs.

"In March 1756, and of course long after all apprehension of a search had ceased, information having been given to the commanding officer at Fraserburgh, that Lord Pitsligo was at that moment at the house of Auchiries, it was acted upon with so much promptness and secrecy that the search must have proved successful but for a very singular occurrence. Mrs. Sophia Donaldson, a lady who lived much with the family, repeatedly dreamt, on that particular night, that the house was surrounded by soldiers. Her mind became so haunted with the idea, that she got out of bed, and was walking through the room, in hopes of giving a different current to her thoughts before she lay down again; when, day beginning to dawn, she accidentally looked out at the window as she passed it in traversing the room, and was astonished at actually observing the figures of soldiers among some trees near the house. So completely had all idea of a search been by that time laid asleep, that she supposed they had come to steal poultry—Jacobite poultry-yards affording a safe object of pillage for the English soldiers in those days. Mrs. Sophia was proceeding to rouse the servants, when her sister, having awaked, and inquiring what was the matter, and being told of soldiers near the house, exclaimed in great alarm, that she feared they wanted something more than hens. She begged Mrs. Sophia to look out at a window on the other side of the house, when not only were soldiers seen in that direction, but also an officer giving instructions by signal, and frequently putting his fingers to his lips, as if enjoining silence. There was now no time to be lost in rousing the family, and all the haste that could be made was scarcely sufficient to hurry the venerable man from his bed into a small recess, behind the wainscot of an adjoining room, which was concealed by a bed, in which a lady, Miss Gordon of Towie, who was there on a visit,

lay, before the soldiers obtained admission.   A
most minute search took place.   The room in
which Lord Pitsligo was concealed did not escape.
Miss Gordon's bed was carefully examined, and
she was obliged to suffer the rude scrutiny of one
of the party, by feeling her chin, to ascertain that
it was not a man in a lady's night-dress.   Before
the soldiers had finished their examination in this
room, the confinement and anxiety increased Lord
Pitsligo's asthma so much, and his breathing became so loud, that it cost Miss Gordon, lying in
bed, much and violent coughing, which she coun-
terfeited, in order to prevent the high breathings
behind the wainscot from being heard.   It may be
easily be conceived what agony she would suffer,
lest, by overdoing her part, she should increase
suspicion, and in fact lead to a discovery.   The
ruse was fortunately successful.   On the search
through the house being given over, Lord Pitsligo
was hastily taken from his confined situation, and
again replaced in bed ; and, as soon as he was able
to speak, his accustomed kindness of heart made
him say to his servant—' James, go and see that
these poor fellows get some breakfast, and a drink
of warm ale, for this is a cold morning ; they are
only doing their duty, and cannot bear me any ill-
will.'   When the family were felicitating each other
on his escape, he pleasantly observed,—' A poor
prize, had they obtained it—an old dying man ! ' "

This was the last attempt made on the part of
government to seize on the persons of any of the
surviving insurgents.   Three years before, Dr.
Archibald Cameron, a brother of Locheill, having clandestinely revisited Scotland, was arrested,
tried, and executed for high treason at Tyburn.
The government was generally blamed for this act
of severity, which was considered rather to have
been dictated by revenge than required for the
public safety.   It is, however, probable that they
might have had secret information of certain
negotiations which were still conducted in the

Highlands by the agents of the Stuart family, and
that they considered it necessary, by one terrible
example, to overawe the insurrectionary spirit.
This I believe to have been the real motive of an
execution which otherwise could not have been
palliated; and, in the case of Lord Pitsligo, it is
quite possible that the zeal of a partisan may have
led him to take a step which would not have been
approved of by the ministry. After the lapse of so
many years, and after so many scenes of judicial
bloodshed, the nation would have turned in dis-
gust from the spectacle of an old man, whose
private life was not only blameless, but exemplary,
dragged to the scaffold, and forced to lay down
his head in expiation of a doubtful crime : and
this view derives corroboration from the fact that,
shortly afterwards, Lord Pitsligo was tacitly permitted to return to the society of his friends,
without further notice or persecution.

Dr. King, the Principal of St. Mary's Hall,
Oxford, has borne the following testimony to the
character of Lord Pitsligo. " Whoever is so happy,
either from his natural disposition, or his good
judgment, constantly to observe St. Paul's precept,
' to speak evil of no one,' will certainly acquire
the love and esteem of the whole community of
which he is a member. But such a man is the
rara avis in terris ; and, among all my acquaintance, I have known only one person to whom I
can with truth assign this character. The person
I mean is the present Lord Pitsligo of Scotland.
I not only never heard this gentleman speak an
ill word of any man living, but I always observed
him ready to defend any other person who was ill
spoken of in his company. If the person accused
were of his acquaintance, my Lord Pitsligo would
always find something good to say of him as a
counterpoise. If he were a stranger, and quite
unknown to him, my Lord would urge in his
defence the general corruption of manners, and
the frailties and infirmities of human nature.

"It is no wonder that such an excellent man, who, besides, is a polite scholar, and has many other great and good qualities, should be universally admired and beloved—insomuch, that I persuade myself he has not one enemy in the world. At least, to this general esteem and affection for his person, his preservation must be owing; for since his attainder he has never removed far from his own house, protected by men of different principles, and unsought for and unmolested by government." To which eulogy it might be added, by those who have the good fortune to know his representatives, that the virtues here acknowledged seem hereditary in the family of Pitsligo.

The venerable old nobleman was permitted to remain without molestation at the residence of his son, during the latter years of an existence protracted to the extreme verge of human life. And so, says the author of his memoirs, "In this happy frame of mind,—calm and full of hope,—the saintly man continued to the last, with his reason unclouded, able to study his favourite volume, enjoying the comforts of friendship, and delighting in the consolations of religion, till he gently 'fell asleep in Jesus.' He died on the 21st of December 1762, in the eighty-fifth year of his age; and to his surviving friends the recollection of the misfortunes which had accompanied him through his long life was painfully awakened even in the closing scene of his mortal career—as his son had the mortification to be indebted to a stranger, now the proprietor of his ancient inheritance by purchase from the crown, for permission to lay his father's honoured remains in the vault which contained the ashes of his family for many generations."

Such a character as this is well worthy of remembrance; and Lord Pitsligo has just title to be called the last of the old Scottish Cavaliers. I trust that, in adapting the words of the following little ballad to a well-known English air, I have committed no unpardonable larceny.

THE OLD SCOTTISH CAVALIER.

I.

COME listen to another song,
　Should make your heart beat high,
Bring crimson to your forehead,
　And the lustre to your eye ;—
It is a song of olden time,
　Of days long since gone by,
And of a Baron stout and bold
　As e'er wore sword on thigh !
　　　Like a brave old Scottish cavalier,
　　　　All of the olden time !

II.

He kept his castle in the north,
　Hard by the thundering Spey ;
And a thousand vassals dwelt around,
　All of his kindred they.
And not a man of all that clan
　Had ever ceased to pray
For the Royal race they loved so well,
　Though exiled far away
　　　From the steadfast Scottish cavaliers,
　　　　All of the olden time !

III.

His father drew the righteous sword
　For Scotland and her claims,
Among the loyal gentlemen
　And chiefs of ancient names

Who swore to fight or fall beneath
  The standard of King James,
And died at Killiecrankie pass
  With the glory of the Græmes ;
    Like a true old Scottish cavalier,
    All of the olden time !

IV.

He never owned the foreign rule,
  No master he obeyed,
But kept his clan in peace at home,
  From foray and from raid ;
And when they asked him for his oath,
  He touched his glittering blade,
And pointed to his bonnet blue,
  That bore the white cockade :
    Like a leal old Scottish cavalier,
    All of the olden time !

V.

At length the news ran through the land—
  THE PRINCE had come again !
That night the fiery cross was sped
  O'er mountain and through glen ;
And our old Baron rose in might,
  Like a lion from his den,
And rode away across the hills
  To Charlie and his men,
    With the valiant Scottish cavaliers,
    All of the olden time !

VI.

He was the first that bent the knee
  When THE STANDARD waved abroad,
He was the first that charged the foe
  On Preston's bloody sod ;
And ever, in the van of fight,
  The foremost still he trod,

Until, on bleak Culloden's heath,
He gave his soul to God,
Like a good old Scottish cavalier,
All of the olden time!

VII.

Oh! never shall we know again
A heart so stout and true—
The olden times have passed away,
And weary are the new:
The fair White Rose has faded
From the garden where it grew,
And no fond tears save those of heaven
The glorious bed bedew
Of the last old Scottish cavalier,
All of the olden time!

MISCELLANEOUS POEMS.

BLIND OLD MILTON.

PLACE me once more, my daughter, where the sun
May shine upon my old and time-worn head,
For the last time, perchance.   My race is run ;
And soon amidst the ever-silent dead
I must repose, it may be, half forgot.
Yes ! I have broke the hard and bitter bread
For many a year, with those who trembled not
To buckle on their armour for the fight,
And set themselves against the tyrant's lot ;
And I have never bowed me to his might,
Nor knelt before him—for I bear within
My heart the sternest consciousness of right,
And that perpetual hate of gilded sin
Which made me what I am ; and though the stain
Of poverty be on me, yet I win
More honour by it, than the blinded train
Who hug their willing servitude, and bow
Unto the weakest and the most profane.
Therefore, with unencumbered soul I go
Before the footstool of my Maker, where
I hope to stand as undebased as now !

Child ! is the sun abroad ?   I feel my hair
Borne up and wafted by the gentle wind,
I feel the odours that perfume the air,
And hear the rustling of the leaves behind.
Within my heart I picture them, and then
I almost can forget that I am blind,
And old, and hated by my fellow-men.
Yet would I fain once more behold the grace
Of nature ere I die, and gaze again

Upon her living and rejoicing face—
Fain would I see thy countenance, my child,
My comforter! I feel thy dear embrace—
I hear thy voice, so musical and mild,
The patient, sole interpreter, by whom
So many years of sadness are beguiled ;
For it hath made my small and scanty room
Peopled with glowing visions of the past.
But I will calmly bend me to my doom,
And wait the hour which is approaching fast,
When triple light shall stream upon mine eyes,
And heaven itself be opened up at last
To him who dared foretell its mysteries.
I have had visions in this drear eclipse
Of outward consciousness, and clomb the skies,
Striving to utter with my earthly lips
What the diviner soul had half divined,
Even as the Saint in his Apocalypse
Who saw the inmost glory, where enshrined
Sat he who fashioned glory.   This hath driven
All outward strife and tumult from my mind,
And humbled me, until I have forgiven
My bitter enemies, and only seek
To find the straight and narrow path to heaven.

Yet I am weak—oh ! how entirely weak,
For one who may not love nor suffer more !
Sometimes unbidden tears will wet my cheek,
And my heart bound as keenly as of yore,
Responsive to a voice, now hushed to rest,
Which made the beautiful Italian shore,
In all its pomp of summer vineyards drest,
An Eden and a Paradise to me.
Do the sweet breezes from the balmy west
Still murmur through thy groves, Parthenope,
In search of odours from the orange bowers ?
Still on thy slopes of verdure does the bee
Cull her rare honey from the virgin flowers ?
And Philomel her plaintive chaunt prolong
'Neath skies more calm and more serene than ours,
Making the summer one perpetual song ?

Art thou the same as when in manhood's pride
I walked in joy thy grassy meads among,
With that fair youthful vision by my side,
In whose bright eyes I looked—and not in vain?
O my adorèd angel! O my bride!
Despite of years, and woe, and want, and pain,
My soul yearns back towards thee, and I seem
To wander with thee, hand in hand, again,
By the bright margin of that flowing stream.
I hear again thy voice, more silver-sweet
Than fancied music floating in a dream,
Possess my being; from afar I greet
The waving of thy garments in the glade,
And the light rustling of thy fairy feet—
What time as one half eager, half afraid,
Love's burning secret faltered on my tongue,
And tremulous looks and broken words betrayed
The secret of the heart from whence they sprung.
Ah me! the earth that rendered thee to heaven
Gave up an angel beautiful and young,
Spotless and pure as snow when freshly driven:
A bright Aurora for the starry sphere
Where all is love, and even life forgiven.
Bride of immortal beauty—ever dear!
Dost thou await me in thy blest abode?
While I, Tithonus-like, must linger here,
And count each step along the rugged road;
A phantom, tottering to a long-made grave,
And eager to lay down my weary load!

I, who was fancy's lord, am fancy's slave.
Like the low murmurs of the Indian shell
Ta'en from its coral bed beneath the wave,
Which, unforgetful of the ocean's swell,
Retains within its mystic urn the hum
Heard in the sea-grots where the Nereids dwell—
Old thoughts still haunt me—unawares they come
Between me and my rest, nor can I make
Those aged visitors of sorrow dumb.
Oh, yet awhile, my feeble soul, awake!
Nor wander back with sullen steps again;

For neither pleasant pastime canst thou take
In such a journey, nor endure the pain.
The phantoms of the past are dead for thee;
So let them ever uninvoked remain,
And be thou calm, till death shall set thee free.
Thy flowers of hope expanded long ago,
Long since their blossoms withered on the tree:
No second spring can come to make them blow,
But in the silent winter of the grave
They lie with blighted love and buried woe.

I did not waste the gifts which nature gave,
Nor slothful lay in the Circéan bower;
Nor did I yield myself the willing slave
Of lust for pride, for riches, or for power.
No! in my heart a nobler spirit dwelt;
For constant was my faith in manhood's dower;
Man—made in God's own image—and I felt
How of our own accord we courted shame,
Until to idols like ourselves we knelt,
And so renounced the great and glorious claim
Of freedom, our immortal heritage.
I saw how bigotry, with spiteful aim,
Smote at the searching eyesight of the sage,
How error stole behind the steps of truth,
And cast delusion on the sacred page.
So, as a champion, even in early youth
I waged my battle with a purpose keen;
Nor feared the hand of terror, nor the tooth
Of serpent jealousy. And I have been
With starry Galileo in his cell,
That wise magician with the brow serene,
Who fathomed space; and I have seen him tell
The wonders of the planetary sphere,
And trace the ramparts of heaven's citadel
On the cold flag-stones of his dungeon drear.
And I have walked with Hampden and with Vane—
Names once so gracious to an English ear—
In days that never may return again.
My voice, though not the loudest, hath been heard
Whenever freedom raised her cry of pain,

And the faint effort of the humble bard
Hath roused up thousands from their lethargy,
To speak in words of thunder.   What reward
Was mine, or theirs?   It matters not ; for I
Am but a leaf cast on the whirling tide,
Without a hope or wish, except to die.
But truth, asserted once, must still abide,
Unquenchable, as are those fiery springs
Which day and night gush from the mountain-side,
Perpetual meteors girt with lambent wings,
Which the wild tempest tosses to and fro,
But cannot conquer with the force it brings.

Yet I, who ever felt another's woe
More keenly than my own untold distress ;
I, who have battled with the common foe,
And broke for years the bread of bitterness ;
Who never yet abandoned or betrayed
The trust vouchsafed me, nor have ceased to bless,
Am left alone to wither in the shade,
A weak old man, deserted by his kind—
Whom none will comfort in his age, nor aid !

Oh, let me not repine !   A quiet mind,
Conscious and upright, needs no other stay ;
Nor can I grieve for what I leave behind,
In the rich promise of eternal day.
Henceforth to me the world is dead and gone,
Its thorns unfelt, its roses cast away :
And the old pilgrim, weary and alone,
Bowed down with travel, at his Master's gate
Now sits, his task of life-long labour done,
Thankful for rest, although it comes so late,
After sore journey through this world of sin,
In hope, and prayer, and wistfulness to wait,
Until the door shall ope, and let him in.

HERMOTIMUS.

HERMOTIMUS, the hero of this ballad, was a philosopher, or rather a prophet, of Clazomenæ, who possessed the faculty, now claimed by the animal-magnetists, of effecting a voluntary separation between his soul and body; for the former could wander to any part of the universe, and even hold intercourse with supernatural beings, whilst the senseless frame remained at home. Hermotimus, however, was not insensible to the risk attendant upon this disunion; since, before attempting any of these aërial flights, he took the precaution to warn his wife, lest, ere the return of his soul, the body should be rendered an unfit or useless receptacle. This accident, which he so much dreaded, at length occurred; for the lady, wearied out by a succession of trances, each of longer duration than the preceding, one day committed his body to the flames, and thus effectually put a stop to such unconnubial conduct. He received divine honours at Clazomenæ, but must nevertheless remain as a terrible example and warning to all husbands who carry their scientific or spiritual pursuits so far as to neglect their duty to their wives.

It is somewhat curious that Hermotimus is not the only person (putting the disciples of Mesmer and Dupotet altogether out of the question) who has possessed this miraculous power. Another and much later instance is recorded by Dr. George Cheyne, in his work entitled *The English Malady, or a Treatise of Nervous Diseases*, as having come under his own observation; and, as this case is exactly similar to that of the Prophet, it may amuse the reader to see how far an ancient fable may be illustrated, and in part explained, by the records of modern science. Dr. Cheyne's patient was probably cataleptic; but the worthy physician must be allowed to tell his own story.

"Colonel Townshend, a gentleman of honour and integrity, had for many years been afflicted with a nephritic complaint. His illness increasing, and his strength decaying, he came from Bristol to Bath in a litter, in autumn, and lay at the Bell Inn. Dr. Baynard and I were called to him, and attended him twice a-day; but his vomitings continuing still incessant and obstinate against all remedies, we despaired of his recovery. While he was in this condition, he sent for us one morning; we waited on him with Mr. Skrine, his apothecary. We found his senses clear, and his mind calm: his nurse and several servants were about him. He told us he had sent for us to give him an account of an odd sensation he had for some time observed and felt in himself; which was, that, by composing himself, *he could die or expire when he pleased;* and yet by an effort, or somehow, he could come to life again, which he had sometimes tried before he sent for us. We heard this with surprise; but, as it was not to be accounted for upon common principles, we could hardly believe the fact as he related it, much less give any account of it; unless he should please to make the experiment before us, which we were unwilling he should do, lest, in his weak condition, he might carry it too far. He continued to talk very distinctly and sensibly above a quarter of an hour about this surprising sensation, and insisted so much on our seeing the trial made, that we were at last forced to comply. We all three felt his pulse first—it was distinct, though small and thready, and his heart had its usual beating. He composed himself on his back, and lay in a still posture for some time: while I held his right hand,

Dr. Baynard laid his hand on his heart, and Mr. Skrine held a clean looking-glass to his mouth. I found his pulse sink gradually, till at last I could not find any by the most exact and nice touch. Dr. Baynard could not feel the least motion in his heart, nor Mr. Skrine the least soil of breath on the bright mirror he held to his mouth; then each of us by turns examined his arm, heart, and breath, but could not, by the nicest scrutiny, discover the least symptom of life in him. We reasoned a long time about this odd appearance as well as we could, and all of us judging it inexplicable and unaccountable; and, finding he still continued in that condition, we began to conclude that he had indeed carried the experiment too far; and at last were satisfied he was actually dead, and were just ready to leave him. This continued about half an hour. As we were going away, we observed some motion about the body; and, upon examination, found his pulse and the motion of his heart gradually returning. He began to breathe gently and speak softly. We were all astonished to the last degree at this unexpected change; and, after some further conversation with him, and among ourselves, went away fully satisfied as to all the particulars of this fact, but confounded and puzzled, and not able to form any rational scheme that might account for it."

I.

"Wilt not lay thee down in quiet slumber?
  Weary dost thou seem, and ill at rest;
Sleep will bring thee dreams in starry number—
  Let him come to thee and be thy guest.
      Midnight now is past—
      Husband! come at last—
  Lay thy throbbing head upon my breast."

II.

"Weary am I, but my soul is waking;
    Fain I'd lay me gently by thy side,
But my spirit then, its home forsaking,
    Through the realms of space would wander
        wide—
            Everything forgot,
            What would be thy lot,
    If I came not back to thee, my bride?

III.

"Music, like the lute of young Apollo,
    Vibrates even now within mine ear;
Soft and silver voices bid me follow,
    Yet my soul is dull and will not hear.
            Waking it will stay:
            Let me watch till day—
    Fainter will they come, and disappear."

IV.

"Speak not thus to me, my own—my dearest,
    These are but the phantoms of thy brain;
Nothing can befall thee which thou fearest,
    Thou shalt wake to love and life again.
            Were this sleep thy last,
            I should hold thee fast,
    Thou shouldst strive against me but in vain.

V.

"Eros will protect us, and will hover,
    Guardian-like, above thee all the night,
Jealous of thee, as of some fond lover
    Chiding back the rosy-fingered light—
            He will be thine aid:
            Canst thou feel afraid
    When *his* torch above us burneth bright?

VI.

"Lo! the cressets of the night are waning—
    Old Orion hastens from the sky;

Only thou of all things art remaining
  Unrefreshed by slumber—thou and I.
        Sound and sense are still ;
        Even the distant rill
Murmurs fainter now, and languidly.

VII.

"Come and rest thee, husband !"—And no longer
  Could the young man that fond call resist :
Vainly was he warned, for love was stronger—
  Warmly did he press her to his breast.
        Warmly met she his ;
        Kiss succeeded kiss,
Till their eyelids closed with sleep oppressed.

VIII.

Soon Aurora left her early pillow,
  And the heavens grew rosy-rich, and rare ;
Laughed the dewy plain and glassy billow,
  For the Golden God himself was there ;
        And the vapour-screen
        Rose the hills between,
Steaming up, like incense, in the air.

IX.

O'er her husband sate Ione bending—
  Marble-like and marble-hued he lay ;
Underneath her raven locks descending,
  Paler seemed his face, and ashen gray,
        And so white his brow—
        White and cold as snow—
"Husband! Gods! his soul hath passed away !"

X.

Raise ye up the pile with gloomy shadow—
  Heap it with the mournful cypress-bough !—
And they raised the pile upon the meadow,
  And they heaped the mournful cypress too ;
        And they laid the dead
        On his funeral bed,
And they kindled up the flames below.

XI.

Swiftly rose they, and the corse surrounded,
    Spreading out a pall into the air ;
And the sharp and sudden crackling sounded
    Mournfully to all the watchers there.
        Soon their force was spent,
        And the body blent
    With the embers' slow-expiring glare.

XII.

Night again was come ; but oh, how lonely
    To the mourner did that night appear !
Peace nor rest it brought, but sorrow only,
    Vain repinings and unwonted fear.
        Dimly burned the lamp—
        Chill the air and damp—
    And the winds without were moaning drear.

XIII.

Hush ! a voice in solemn whispers speaking,
    Breaks within the twilight of the room ;
And Ione, loud and wildly shrieking,
    Starts and gazes through the ghastly gloom.
        Nothing sees she there—
        All is empty air,
    All is empty as a rifled tomb.

XIV.

Once again the voice beside her sounded,
    Low, and faint, and solemn was its tone—
" Nor by form or shade am I surrounded,
    Fleshly home and dwelling have I none.
        They are passed away—
        Woe is me ! to-day
    Hath robbed me of myself, and made me lone.

XV.

" Vainly were the words of parting spoken ;
    Evermore must Charon turn from me.

Still my thread of life remains unbroken,
 And unbroken ever it must be ;
  Only they may rest
  Whom the Fates' behest
From their mortal mansion setteth free.

XVI.

" I have seen the robes of Hermes glisten—
 Seen him wave afar his serpent-wand ;
But to me the Herald would not listen—
 When the dead swept by at his command,
  Not with that pale crew
  Durst I venture too—
Ever shut for me the quiet land.

XVII.

" Day and night before the dreary portal,
 Phantom-shapes, the guards of Hades, lie ;
None of heavenly kind, nor yet of mortal,
 May unchallenged pass the warders by.
  None that path may go,
  If he cannot show
His last passport to eternity.

XVIII.

" Cruel was the spirit-power thou gavest—
 Fatal, O Apollo, was thy love !
Pythian ! Archer ! brightest God and bravest,
 Hear, O hear me from thy throne above !
  Let me not, I pray,
  Thus be cast away :
Plead for me—thy slave—O plead to Jove !

XIX.

" I have heard thee with the Muses singing—
 Heard that full melodious voice of thine,
Silver-clear throughout the ether ringing—
 Seen thy locks in golden clusters shine ;
  And thine eye, so bright
  With its innate light,
Hath ere now been bent so low as mine.

XX.

" Hast thou lost the wish—the will—to cherish
　Those who trusted in thy godlike power?
Hyacinthus did not wholly perish !
　Still he lives, the firstling of thy bower ;
　　　Still he feels thy rays,
　　　Fondly meets thy gaze,
　Though but now the spirit of a flower.

XXI.

" Hear me, Phœbus ! Hear me and deliver !
　Lo ! the morning breaketh from afar—
God ! thou comest bright and great as ever—
　Night goes back before thy burning car ;
　　　All her lamps are gone—
　　　Lucifer alone
　Lingers still for thee—the blessed star !

XXII.

" Hear me, Phœbus ! "—And therewith descended
　Through the window-arch a glory-gleam,
All effulgent—and with music blended,
　For such solemn sounds arose as stream
　　　From the Memnon-lyre,
　　　When the morning fire
　Gilds the giant's forehead with its beam.

XXIII.

" Thou hast heard thy servant's prayer, Apollo,
　Thou dost call me, mighty God of Day !
Fare-thee-well, Ione ! "—And more hollow
　Came the phantom-voice, then died away.
　　　When the slaves arose,
　　　Not in calm repose—
　Not in sleep, but death, their mistress lay.

H

ŒNONE.

On the holy mount of Ida,
  Where the pine and cypress grow,
Sate a young and lovely woman,
  Weeping ever, weeping low.
Drearily throughout the forest
  Did the winds of autumn blow,
And the clouds above were flying,
  And Scamander rolled below.

" Faithless Paris ! cruel Paris ! "
  Thus the poor deserted spake—
" Wherefore thus so strangely leave me ?
  Why thy loving bride forsake ?
Why no tender word at parting—
  Why no kiss, no farewell take ?
Would that I could but forget thee—
  Would this throbbing heart might break !

" Is my face no longer blooming ?
  Are my eyes no longer bright ?
Ah ! my tears have made them dimmer,
  And my cheeks are pale and white.
I have wept since early morning,
  I will weep the livelong night ;
Now I long for sullen darkness,
  As I once have longed for light.

" Paris ! canst thou then be cruel ?
  Fair, and young, and brave thou art—
Can it be that in thy bosom
  Lies so cold, so hard a heart ?

Children were we bred together—
  She who bore me suckled thee;
I have been thine old companion,
  When thou hadst no more but me.

" I have watched thee in thy slumbers,
  When the shadow of a dream
Passed across thy smiling features,
  Like the ripple of a stream;
And so sweetly were the visions
  Pictured there with lively grace,
That I half could read their import
  By the changes on thy face.

" When I sang of Ariadne,
  Sang the old and mournful tale,
How her faithless lover, Theseus,
  Left her to lament and wail;
Then thine eyes would fill and glisten,
  Her complaint could soften thee:
Thou hast wept for Ariadne—
  Theseus' self might weep for me!

" Thou may'st find another maiden
  With a fairer face than mine—
With a gayer voice, and sweeter,
  And a spirit liker thine:
For if e'er my beauty bound thee,
  Lost and broken is the spell;
But thou canst not find another
  That will love thee half so well.

" O thou hollow ship that bearest
  Paris o'er the faithless deep!
Wouldst thou leave him on some island
  Where alone the waters weep;
Where no human foot is moulded
  In the wet and yellow sand—
Leave him there, thou hollow vessel!
  Leave him on that lonely land!

"Then his heart will surely soften,
  When his foolish hopes decay,
And his older love rekindle,
  As the new one dies away.
Visionary hills will haunt him,
  Rising from the glassy sea,
And his thoughts will wander homewards
  Unto Ida and to me!

"O! that like a little swallow
  I could reach that lonely spot!
All his errors would be pardoned,
  All the weary past forgot.
Never should he wander from me—
  Never should he more depart;
For these arms would be his prison,
  And his home would be my heart!"

Thus lamented fair Œnone,
  Weeping ever, weeping low,
On the holy mount of Ida,
  Where the pine and cypress grow.
In the self-same hour, Cassandra
  Shrieked her prophecy of woe,
And into the Spartan dwelling
  Did the faithless Paris go.

THE BURIED FLOWER.

IN the silence of my chamber,
  When the night is still and deep,
And the drowsy heave of ocean
  Mutters in its charmèd sleep,

Oft I hear the angel-voices
  That have thrilled me long ago,—
Voices of my lost companions,
  Lying deep beneath the snow.

O, the garden I remember,
  In the gay and sunny spring,
When our laughter made the thickets
  And the arching alleys ring!

O the merry burst of gladness!
  O the soft and tender tone!
O the whisper never uttered
  Save to one fond ear alone!

O the light of life that sparkled
  In those bright and bounteous eyes!
O the blush of happy beauty,
  Tell-tale of the heart's surprise!

O the radiant light that girdled
  Field and forest, land and sea,
When we all were young together,
  And the earth was new to me!

Where are now the flowers we tended?
  Withered, broken, branch and stem;
Where are now the hopes we cherished?
  Scattered to the winds with them.

For ye, too, were flowers, ye dear ones !
  Nursed in hope and reared in love,
Looking fondly ever upward
  To the clear blue heaven above :

Smiling on the sun that cheered us,
  Rising lightly from the rain,
Never folding up your freshness
  Save to give it forth again :

Never shaken, save by accents
  From a tongue that was not free,
As the modest blossom trembles
  At the wooing of the bee.

O ! 'tis sad to lie and reckon
  All the days of faded youth,
All the vows that we believed in,
  All the words we spoke in truth.

Severed—were it severed only
  By an idle thought of strife,
Such as time might knit together ;
  Not the broken chord of life !

O my heart ! that once so truly
  Kept another's time and tune,
Heart, that kindled in the spring-tide,
  Look around thee in the noon.

Where are they who gave the impulse
  To thy earliest thought and flow ?
Look around the ruined garden—
  All are withered, dropped, or low !

Seek the birth-place of the lily,
  Dearer to the boyish dream
Than the golden cups of Eden,
  Floating on its slumbrous stream ;

Never more shalt thou behold her—
  She, the noblest, fairest, best:
She that rose in fullest beauty,
  Like a queen, above the rest.

Only still I keep her image
  As a thought that cannot die;
He who raised the shade of Helen
  Had no greater power than I.

O! I fling my spirit backward,
  And I pass o'er years of pain;
All I loved is rising round me,
  All the lost returns again.

Blow, for ever blow, ye breezes,
  Warmly as ye did before!
Bloom again, ye happy gardens,
  With the radiant tints of yore!

Warble out in spray and thicket,
  All ye choristers unseen;
Let the leafy woodland echo
  With an anthem to its queen!

Lo! she cometh in her beauty,
  Stately with a Juno grace,
Raven locks, Madonna-braided
  O'er her sweet and blushing face:

Eyes of deepest violet, beaming
  With the love that knows not shame—
Lips, that thrill my inmost being
  With the utterance of a name.

And I bend the knee before her,
  As a captive ought to bow,—
Pray thee, listen to my pleading,
  Sovereign of my soul art thou!

O my dear and gentle lady,
   Let me show thee all my pain,
Ere the words that late were prisoned
   Sink into my heart again.

Love, they say, is very fearful
   Ere its curtain be withdrawn,
Trembling at the thought of error
   As the shadows scare the fawn.

Love hath bound me to thee, lady,
   Since the well-remembered day
When I first beheld thee coming
   In the light of lustrous May.

Not a word I dared to utter—
   More than he who, long ago,
Saw the heavenly shapes descending
   Over Ida's slopes of snow :

When a low and solemn music
   Floated through the listening grove,
And the throstle's song was silenced,
   And the cloling of the dove :

When immortal beauty opened
   All its grace to mortal sight,
And the awe of worship blended
   With the throbbing of delight.

As the shepherd stood before them
   Trembling in the Phrygian dell,
Even so my soul and being
   Owned the magic of the spell ;

And I watched thee ever fondly,
   Watched thee, dearest ! from afar,
With the mute and humble homage
   Of the Indian to a star.

Thou wert still the Lady Flora
　In her morning garb of bloom ;
Where thou wert was light and glory,
　Where thou wert not, dearth and gloom.

So for many a day I followed
　For a long and weary while,
Ere my heart rose up to bless thee
　For the yielding of a smile,—

Ere thy words were few and broken
　As they answered back to mine,
Ere my lips had power to thank thee
　For the gift vouchsafed by thine.

Then a mighty gush of passion
　Through my inmost being ran ;
Then my older life was ended,
　And a dearer course began.

Dearer !—O, I cannot tell thee
　What a load was swept away,
What a world of doubt and darkness
　Faded in the dawning day !

All my error, all my weakness,
　All my vain delusions fled :
Hope again revived, and gladness
　Waved its wings above my head.

Like the wanderer of the desert,
　When, across the dreary sand,
Breathes the perfume from the thickets
　Bordering on the promised land ;

When afar he sees the palm-trees
　Cresting o'er the lonely well,
When he hears the pleasant tinkle
　Of the distant camel's bell :

So a fresh and glad emotion
    Rose within my swelling breast,
And I hurried swiftly onwards
    To the haven of my rest.

Thou wert there with word and welcome,
    With thy smile so purely sweet;
And I laid my heart before thee,
    Laid it, darling, at thy feet!—

O ye words that sound so hollow
    As I now recall your tone!
What are ye but empty echoes
    Of a passion crushed and gone?

Wherefore should I seek to kindle
    Light, when all around is gloom?
Wherefore should I raise a phantom
    O'er the dark and silent tomb?

Early wert thou taken, Mary!
    In thy fair and glorious prime,
Ere the bees had ceased to murmur
    Through the umbrage of the lime.

Buds were blowing, waters flowing,
    Birds were singing on the tree,
Every thing was bright and glowing
    When the angels came for thee.

Death had laid aside his terror,
    And he found thee calm and mild,
Lying in thy robes of whiteness,
    Like a pure and stainless child.

Hardly had the mountain violet
    Spread its blossoms on the sod,
Ere they laid the turf above thee,
    And thy spirit rose to God.

Early wert thou taken, Mary !
  And I know 'tis vain to weep—
Tears of mine can never wake thee
  From thy sad and silent sleep.

O away ! my thoughts are earthward !
  Not asleep, my love, art thou !
Dwelling in the land of glory
  With the saints and angels now.

Brighter, fairer far than living,
  With no trace of woe or pain,
Robed in everlasting beauty,
  Shall I see thee once again,

By the light that never fadeth,
  Underneath eternal skies,
When the dawn of resurrection
  Breaks o'er deathless Paradise.

THE OLD CAMP.

WRITTEN IN A ROMAN FORTIFICATION
IN BAVARIA.

I.

THERE is a cloud before the sun,
  The wind is hushed and still,
And silently the waters run
  Beneath the sombre hill.
The sky is dark in every place,
  As is the earth below :
Methinks it wore the self-same face
  Two thousand years ago.

II.

No light is on the ancient wall,
  No light upon the mound ;
The very trees, so thick and tall,
  Cast gloom, not shade, around.
So silent is the place and cold,
  So far from human ken,
It hath a look that makes me old,
  And spectres time again.

III.

I listen, half in thought, to hear
  The Roman trumpet blow—
I search for glint of helm and spear
  Amidst the forest bough :
And armour rings, and voices swell—
  I hear the legion's tramp,
And mark the lonely sentinel
  Who guards the lonely camp.

IV.

Methinks I have no other home,
　No other hearth to find ;
For nothing save the thought of Rome
　Is stirring in my mind.
And all that I have heard or dreamed,
　And all I had forgot,
Are rising up, as though they seemed
　The household of the spot.

V.

And all the names that Romans knew
　Seem just as known to me,
As if I were a Roman too—
　A Roman born and free :
And I could rise at Cæsar's name,
　As though it were a charm
To draw sharp lightning from the tame,
　And brace the coward's arm.

VI.

And yet, if yonder sky were blue,
　And earth were sunny gay,
If nature wore the summer hue
　That decked her yesterday,
The mound, the trench, the rampart's space,
　Would move me nothing more
Than many a sweet sequestred place
　That I have marked before.

VII.

I could not feel the breezes bring
　Rich odours from the trees ;
I could not hear the linnets sing,
　And think on themes like these.
The painted insects as they pass
　In swift and motley strife,
The very lizard in the grass
　Would scare me back to life.

VIII.

Then is the past so gloomy now
　　That it may never bear
The open smile of nature's brow,
　　Or meet the sunny air?
I know not that—but joy is power,
　　However short it last·;
And joy befits the present hour,
　　If sadness fits the past.

DANUBE AND THE EUXINE.

"DANUBE, Danube! wherefore com'st thou
  Red and raging to my caves?
Wherefore leap thy swollen waters
  Madly through the broken waves?
Wherefore is thy tide so sullied
  With a hue unknown to me;
Wherefore dost thou bring pollution
  To the old and sacred sea?"

"Ha! rejoice, old Father Euxine!
  I am brimming full and red;
Noble tidings do I carry
  From my distant channel-bed.
I have been a Christian river
  Dull and slow this many a year,
Rolling down my torpid waters
  Through a silence morne and drear;
Have not felt the tread of armies
  Trampling on my reedy shore;
Have not heard the trumpet calling,
  Or the cannon's gladsome roar;
Only listened to the laughter
  From the village and the town,
And the church-bells, ever jangling,
  As the weary day went down.
So I lay and sorely pondered
  On the days long since gone by,
When my old primæval forests
  Echoed to the war-man's cry;
When the race of Thor and Odin
  Held their battles by my side,

And the blood of man was mingling
   Warmly with my chilly tide.
Father Euxine! thou rememb'rest
   How I brought thee tribute then—
Swollen corpses, gashed and gory,
   Heads and limbs of slaughter'd men?
Father Euxine! be thou joyful!
   I am running red once more—
Not with heathen blood, as early,
   But with gallant Christian gore!
For the old times are returning,
   And the Cross is broken down,
And I hear the tocsin sounding
   In the village and the town;
And the glare of burning cities
   Soon shall light me on my way—
Ha! my heart is big and jocund
   With the draught I drank to-day.
Ha! I feel my strength awakened,
   And my brethren shout to me;
Each is leaping red and joyous
   To his own awaiting sea.
Rhine and Elbe are plunging downward
   Through their wild anarchic land,
Everywhere are Christians falling
   By their brother Christians' hand!
Yea, the old times are returning,
   And the olden gods are here!
Take my tribute, Father Euxine,
   To thy waters dark and drear.
Therefore come I with my torrents,
   Shaking castle, crag, and town;
Therefore, with the shout of thunder,
   Sweep I herd and herdsman down;
Therefore leap I to thy bosom,
   With a loud triumphal roar—
Greet me, greet me, Father Euxine—
   I am Christian stream no more!"

THE SCHEIK OF SINAI IN 1830.

FROM THE GERMAN OF FREILIGRATH.

I.

"LIFT me without the tent, I say,—
  Me and my ottoman,—
I'll see the messenger myself!
  It is the caravan
    From Africa, thou sayest,
      And they bring us news of war?
Draw me without the tent, and quick!
  As at the desert well
The freshness of the purling brook
  Delights the tired gazelle,
    So pant I for the voice of him
      That cometh from afar!"

II.

The Scheik was lifted from his tent,
  And thus outspake the Moor:—
"I saw, old Chief, the Tricolor
  On Algiers' topmost tower—
    Upon its battlements the silks
      Of Lyons flutter free.
Each morning, in the market-place,
  The muster-drum is beat,
And to the war-hymn of Marseilles
  The squadrons pace the street.
    The armament from Toulon sailed:
      The Franks have crossed the sea.

III.

" Towards the south, the columns marched
  Beneath a cloudless sky :
Their weapons glittered in the blaze
  Of the sun of Barbary ;
    And with the dusty desert sand
      Their horses' manes were white.
The wild marauding tribes dispersed
  In terror of their lives ;
They fled unto the mountains
  With their children and their wives,
    And urged the clumsy dromedary
      Up the Atlas' height.

IV.

" The Moors have ta'en their vantage-ground,
  The volleys thunder fast—
The dark defile is blazing
  Like a heated oven-blast ;
    The lion hears the strange turmoil,
      And leaves his mangled prey—
No place was that for him to feed ;
  And thick and loud the cries,
Feu !—Allah ! Allah !—En avant !
  In mingled discord rise ;
    The Franks have reached the summit—
      They have won the victory !

V.

" With bristling steel, upon the top
  The victors take their stand :
Beneath their feet, with all its towns,
  They see the promised land—
    From Tunis, even unto Fez,
      From Atlas to the seas.
The cavaliers alight to gaze,
  And gaze full well they may,

Where countless minarets stand up
So solemnly and gray,
Amidst the dark-green masses
Of the flowering myrtle-trees.

VI.

"The almond blossoms in the vale;
The aloe from the rock
Throws out its long and prickly leaves,
Nor dreads the tempest's shock:
A blessed land, I ween, is that,
Though luckless is its Bey.
There lies the sea—beyond lies France!
Her banners in the air
Float proudly and triumphantly—
A salvo! come, prepare!
And loud and long the mountains rang
With that glad artillery."

VII.

"'Tis they!" exclaimed the aged Scheik.
"I've battled by their side—
I fought beneath the Pyramids!
That day of deathless pride—
Red as thy turban, Moor, that eve,
Was every creek in Nile!
But tell me—" and he griped his hand—
"Their Sultaun. Stranger, say—
His form—his face—his posture, man?'
Thou saw'st him in the fray?
His eye—what wore he?" But the Moor
Sought in his vest awhile.

VIII.

"Their Sultaun, Scheik, remains at home
Within his palace walls:
He sends a Pasha in his stead
To brave the bolts and balls.
He was not there. An Aga burst
For him through Atlas' hold.

Yet I can show thee somewhat too.
  A Frankish Cavalier
Told me his effigy was stamped
  Upon this medal here—
    He gave it me with others
      For an Arab steed I sold."

IX.

The old man took the golden coin :   ·
  Gazed steadfastly awhile,
If that could be the Sultaun
  Whom from the banks of Nile
    He guided o'er the desert path—
      Then sighed and thus spake he—
"'Tis not *his* eye—'tis not *his* brow—
  Another face is there :
I never saw this man before—
  His head is like a pear !
    Take back thy medal, Moor—'tis not
      That which I hoped to see."

EPITAPH OF CONSTANTINE KANARIS.

FROM THE GERMAN OF WILHELM MÜLLER.

I AM Constantine Kanaris:
   I, who lie beneath this stone,
Twice into the air in thunder
   Have the Turkish galleys blown.

In my bed I died—a Christian,
   Hoping straight with Christ to be;
Yet one earthly wish is buried
   Deep within the grave with me—

That upon the open ocean
   When the third Armada came,
They and I had died together,
   Whirled aloft on wings of flame.

Yet 'tis something that they've laid me
   In a land without a stain:
Keep it thus, my God and Saviour,
   Till I rise from earth again!

*

THE REFUSAL OF CHARON.*

FROM THE ROMAIC.

WHY look the distant mountains
   So gloomy and so drear?
Are rain-clouds passing o'er them,
   Or is the tempest near?
No shadow of the tempest
   Is there, nor wind nor rain—
'Tis Charon that is passing by,
   With all his gloomy train.

The young men march before him,
   In all their strength and pride;
The tender little infants,
   They totter by his side;
The old men walk behind him,
   And earnestly they pray—
Both old and young imploring him
   To grant some brief delay.

"O Charon! halt, we pray thee,
   Beside some little town,
Or near some sparkling fountain,
   Where the waters wimple down!
The old will drink and be refreshed,
   The young the disc will fling,
And the tender little children
   Pluck flowers beside the spring."

* According to the superstition of the modern Greeks,
Charon performs the function which their ancestors
assigned to Hermes, of conducting the souls of the
dead to the other world.

" I will not stay my journey,
　　Nor halt by any town,
Near any sparkling fountain,
　　Where the waters wimple down :
The mothers coming to the well .
　　Would know the babes they bore,
The wives would clasp their husbands,
　　Nor could I part them more."

THE END.

BALLANTYNE PRESS : EDINBURGH AND LONDON

www.ingramcontent.com/pod-product-compliance
Lightning Source LLC
Chambersburg PA
CBHW031107020726
47495CB00007B/2095